"JOHNNY ORT...
WITH THE DES...
SANTO CRIST...
—Doroth...
Myster...

JOHNNY ORTIZ: His people had been warriors and hunters, and the Santo Cristo cop would do them proud. He was tracking down a conspiracy of contraband and murder—and going to war against the man behind it all . . .

WALTER HIGGINS: His fellow FBI agents called him a loose cannon. He came to Santo Cristo on a sensitive matter, and one day later he was dead . . .

CASSIE ENRIGHT: Any man would want to be seen with Ortiz's girlfriend—a sharp, black, drop-dead beauty. But Leon Bascomb had his own reasons for becoming friendly with Cassie . . .

LEON BASCOMB: In Santo Cristo he was pure Miami—from his monogrammed shirts to his tasseled loafers. He called himself a businessman, but Johnny was sure he was a killer, maybe more . . .

MOLLIE HIGGINS: "A desert pocket mouse," Johnny called her at first. But the little woman had the heart of a tiger, and she would prove it to her husband's killer . . .

BEN HART: Locals knew not to cross the big, brawny rancher, but an out-of-town crime boss didn't heed the cattleman's warnings . . .

ARTIE GILMORE: He came from Florida packing gold chains and a gun. His job: kill Johnny Oritz . . .

"WHAT A FIND! IT SEEMS THAT WHATEVER RICHARD MARTIN STERN WRITES IS AN IMMEDIATE SUCCESS . . . IN THE CLASSIC STYLE. . . . HE IS A WRITER WHO VALUES TASTE AND STYLE."
—Dorothy B. Hughes, Grand Master Award–winner, Mystery Writers of America

Books by Richard Martin Stern

Death in the Snow
Interloper
Missing Man
Murder in the Walls
Tangled Murders
You Don't Need an Enemy

Published by POCKET BOOKS

INTERLOPER

Richard Martin Stern

POCKET BOOKS

New York   London   Toronto   Sydney   Tokyo   Singapore

An *Original* Publication of POCKET BOOKS

POCKET BOOKS, a division of Simon & Schuster Inc.
1230 Avenue of the Americas, New York, NY 10020

ISBN: 0-671-70018-9

First Pocket Books printing September 1990

10 9 8 7 6 5 4 3 2 1

POCKET and colophon are registered trademarks of Simon & Schuster Inc.

Printed in the U.S.A.

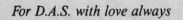

For D.A.S. with love always

————————— 1 —————————

The FBI man, whose name was Walter Higgins, was clearly uncomfortable as he sat in Johnny's office. "Uh," he said, "normally we—ah—prefer to keep matters, sensitive matters, that is, to ourselves until the time comes to make them public. If you see what I mean, Lieutenant?"

Johnny's face showed nothing, and his dark eyes—angry eyes, old Ben Hart had called them—reflected light from the windows like chips of obsidian. Juan Felipe Ortiz, lieutenant, Santo Cristo police, Apache on his mother's side and, as far as he knew, half Hispanic and half Anglo on his father's. "If what you're saying," he said, "is that you Feds like to keep everyone else in the dark, yes, I see exactly what you mean. So?"

"Uh," Higgins said, "down in the city there is a federal magistrate, a hard-nosed—" He hesitated.

"Son of a bitch?" Johnny suggested, still showing no expression.

"You said it, Lieutenant. I didn't. But, yes, you do have the idea. And he, ah, insisted that I touch base with you."

"Before you start poking around on my turf?" Johnny said. He nodded then. "Sensible fellow. Who and what are you interested in in Santo Cristo?"

Higgins hesitated again. "You have a new resident," he said, and tried to leave it there.

"We have quite a few new residents," Johnny said. "Santo Cristo has apparently become an attractive place to live. Which new resident do you have in mind?"

Higgins sighed. "His name is Bascomb, Leon Bascomb. That is not the name he was born with, but it is the name he has used for some time. He has bought a house here."

"Up on Tano Road," Johnny said, "yes. Fifteen fenced acres, a house of about 10,000 square feet, a swimming pool, a guest house, a four-car garage, and a helicopter pad. I understand he paid cash, somewhere on the order of two and a half or three million. The check cleared without question."

"His last residence was Miami," Higgins said. "We are wondering why he moved here."

"Have you asked him?"

Higgins took his time, clearly uncertain what to say next. At last he stood up. "Thank you for your time, Lieutenant. I will tell the magistrate that I did touch base with you." He did not offer to shake hands. "See you around," he said, and walked out.

Johnny sat motionless for a little time, staring at his thoughts. Then he called in Tony Lopez, sergeant, Santo Cristo-born and -bred, large, solid, cheerful. Tony leaned comfortably against the wall and waited.

"Leon Bascomb," Johnny said. "The Feds are interested in him. Why?"

Tony shrugged hugely and spread his hands. When he smiled he showed many white teeth.

"A place that size," Johnny said, "needs help, quite a bit of help. Locals?"

"That," Tony said, "I can answer, *amigo*. He brought his own help all the way from Miami."

"Anglo? Hispanic?"

"Both. And a Filipino cook—chef."

"Have the neighbors complained about the chopper noise?"

The white teeth appeared in a broad smile. "Not yet. But they will. They like to complain."

Johnny nodded. "When they do, we'll pay Mr. Bascomb a visit, no?"

"Seguro que sí," Tony said. His smile was happy, anticipatory.

Leon Bascomb drove a Cadillac coupe, dark gray in color, with tinted windows and windshield. That the glass and the doors were bulletproof was not readily apparent.

Bascomb was close to six feet in height, slim, always impeccably tailored even in monogrammed sleeveless shirts and odd trousers. His hair was dark, worn a trifle long and carefully trimmed. He showed a touch of gray at the temples. He exercised daily and swam laps in his heated pool.

He took season tickets at the Santo Cristo opera and at the chamber music recitals, attended most gallery openings, and donated heavily to the hospital and both the state and private museums. He was careful to wait a few months after his arrival in town before he issued invitations to his first party, which was an informal buffet on a Sunday afternoon with a carefully selected list of forty guests.

The Filipino chef provided the hors d'oeuvres as well as the salads, the whole smoked salmon, the beautifully glazed baked ham, and the platters of imported cheeses. Maids in Mexican dresses passed trays of refreshments. There was subdued music from a mariachi band.

Congressman Mark Hawley came to the party, as did old Ben Hart, who wore, out of politeness for the occasion, a baggy tweed jacket with his usual jeans, flannel shirt, and heeled boots. Looking around at the loaded tables and general decor, Ben said, "What comes next, dancing girls?"

"What'd you expect," Mark Hawley said, "tin plates and beans?"

Johnny Ortiz did not attend the party, nor was he invited. On that Sunday afternoon he was at his desk conferring with an obviously worried special agent in charge from the FBI's big city office 65 miles away.

"Wallace," the FBI man said, and produced his ID. "Our man Higgins touched base with you early last week, I understand, Lieutenant?"

"Those were the words he used," Johnny said, with no special emphasis in his voice. "He mentioned a hard-nosed federal magistrate who had the odd idea that jurisdictional boundaries ought to be respected."

Wallace said somewhat stiffly, "It may seem to you, Lieutenant, that we are at times a trifle . . . high-handed, but I assure you that we cooperate with local officials whenever we can."

"Like now," Johnny said. "So what can I do for you?"

Wallace took a deep breath. "Have you seen Higgins?"

"Not since that day."

"You haven't heard from him?"

"No. And I haven't heard anything about him, either. Has he dropped out of sight?"

"Why do you say that, Lieutenant?"

"Because otherwise I don't think you'd be here asking me questions. When did you hear from him last?" He watched hesitation form on Wallace's face. "Unless, of course," Johnny added, "it's a federal secret."

"No secret, Lieutenant." Wallace's resentment was clear. "He has not checked in since the day he saw you." Again hesitation was plain.

Johnny waited patiently.

"Did he say where he was going?" Wallace said at last as if the question was painful to ask.

"No. He mentioned a man named Bascomb, Leon Bascomb, but that was all."

It was then that the phone on Johnny's desk rang, and he nodded to Wallace in apology as he picked it up. The voice of the sergeant at the front desk said, "I think you'd better take this one, Lieutenant. It's up your alley. Line three."

Johnny nodded again at Wallace and punched the line-three button, listened quietly for a few moments, then hung up with a simple, "Okay. Wait there. Ten minutes."

Looking again at Wallace, it passed through Johnny's mind that sometimes, often enough to make a man wonder, facts and events seemed to mesh, almost as if they had been planned.

"Maybe," he said, "just maybe I have an answer to your questions. There's a body up on Elk Ridge. Three hikers found it and came back down to call it in." He pushed back his chair and stood up. "Coming?" he said, and, turning, walked out to his four-wheel-drive pickup, Wallace right behind him.

There is a badly maintained road up to Elk Ridge that almost demands four-wheel drive. It was late summer and the snows had not yet come to make matters worse. The ridge itself is six miles long, gently undulating between elevations of 10,800 and 11,200 feet. The ridge is below timberline—which at this latitude is 11,500 feet—and is heavily timbered, but in places there are open views of stunning magnificence from the backside of the Sangre de Cristo Mountains rising to over 13,000 feet, across the deep Pecos Valley on the one hand, and on the other, the country falling away for tens of thousands of square miles as it drops into Kansas, Oklahoma, and beyond with no real horizon in sight. The ancient city of Santo Cristo, itself at an elevation of 7,000 feet, is hidden from Elk Ridge by the mountains.

Johnny parked his truck at the end of the road up beside the Jeep the three hikers had driven, and got out. "How far?" he said.

One of the hikers, a man named Martin, young, fresh-faced, a teller in one of the local banks, Johnny seemed to remember, said, "About halfway to Skull Junction." He flushed then, and grinned sheepishly. "We call it that because we found a cow skull there once and stuck it on a tree branch."

"That," Johnny said, nodding, "is the way a lot of places around here got their names." He reached back into the pickup and took the lever-action 30-30 carbine from its rack against the cab window, not out of fear of trouble, merely out of long habit in wild country. "Lead away," he said.

They walked in single file, following the faint trail

that wound among and between towering Ponderosa pines and low brush with here and there a scrub oak and even an occasional Bristlecone pine wearing its vast age with disfigured dignity.

Martin, in the lead, said over his shoulder, "My wife and I come up here sometimes to gather mushrooms." He glanced nervously back at Johnny to see if small talk was out of place.

"Chanterelles," Johnny said, nodding again. "They're good to dry." He walked easily, the carbine held loosely in one hand, his breathing unaffected by the altitude. "Nice place for picnics, too," he added.

"But, God," Martin said, in a new, different voice, "to find a—body! That's so—damned out of place!"

"It always is," Johnny said, and there was no more talk.

The body lay in a clearing, a few hundred feet down the mountainside. Johnny led the way cautiously on the talus slope and, laying the carbine aside, hunkered down to turn the dead man's head enough to see what was left of his face. "Here's your answer," he said to Wallace in a hard, flat voice. "Now you know why Higgins hasn't checked in."

Wallace said softly, "Jesus!" He looked around at the hundreds of square miles of emptiness. "But how did he get here? And why?"

"No tracks," Johnny said. "In talus, there might not be anything plain, but there would be some sign." He was silent for a moment. "And he didn't walk far up here in those shoes." He stood up, carbine in hand again.

Martin said in a hushed voice, "It's as if he dropped from the sky!"

"And that," Johnny said, "just could be it. We may know better when Doc Means has a good look at him." He glanced around. "I'll stay here. You," he said to Wallace, "use the radio in my truck. We want a packhorse. It's too far to carry him. I'll poke around."

Wallace opened his mouth as if to protest, but Johnny cut him off. "Friend," Johnny said, "you're definitely in my jurisdiction now. You take orders instead of giving them. Understood?"

Wallace nodded then, and managed a faint smile. "I take your point, Lieutenant. I will do as you say. Do you want your Doc Means?"

Johnny shook his head. "Doc's too old to scramble around at this elevation. Besides, he's a flatlander."

Doc Means was in his seventies, happily engaged as Santo Cristo's dollar-a-year coroner-pathologist, almost the same occupation he had filled for years at a far more munificent salary back in the crowded East. "You do come up with some dandies," he told Johnny the next day. "I used to think I'd seen it all, but out here you keep adding new wrinkles. Have you any idea what happened to him?"

"You tell me," Johnny said.

Doc looked thoughtful. "They used to stone folks to death," he said finally, "but as far as I know, that went out of style quite a while ago. Otherwise . . ." He spread his hands.

"I think I'm with you," Johnny said, "but spell it out anyway."

"Broken bones," Doc said, "massive internal injuries, and a fractured skull, and as if that weren't enough, he has a bullet in him, too—several of them, as a matter of fact. They were the cause of death. Saul says they're from some kind of automatic weapon." Saul Pentland was the state police technician. Doc shrugged. "I'm no ballistics man."

Johnny said, "What if somebody dropped him out of an aircraft from maybe a thousand feet and he landed on that talus slope. Would that fit?"

Doc opened his mouth in surprise, closed it, and nodded somberly. "Like I said, out here you keep adding new wrinkles."

"Thanks, Doc," Johnny said. "I'll have a talk with Saul."

First, though, Johnny placed a call to Wallace down in the big city to report Doc's findings. "By the way," he added, "he had no gun in his holster, and no ID. I looked."

Wallace's silence was somehow expressive.

Johnny said, "Care to tell me what he was working on?"

"Under the circumstances," Wallace said, "I would, if I knew. And you can believe that."

"Leon Bascomb," Johnny said. "What do you have on him?"

"Very little. Miami businessman. No record. Has money to invest in all kinds of things—banks, new ventures, real estate, you name it."

"Higgins was interested in him."

"Higgins was interested in a lot of people. And he had a habit of keeping things to himself even more than we usually do." Was there a wry smile behind the last words?

"I'll be in touch," Johnny said. He hung up and pushed back his chair. Saul Pentland next, he thought, not with anything particular in mind, merely following a feeling. Feelings, Johnny had long ago decided, frequently had more behind them than you tended at first to understand.

Saul, ex-Dallas Cowboys defensive tackle, bearded

like an ancient prophet and, in his white coat, about the size of a polar bear, was in his lab. "You've talked to Doc?" he said, and listened quietly to Johnny's report.

"I noticed the empty holster, too," Saul said, *"and* the lack of ID. No wallet, no keys, no notebook or pen—and no money. FBI, you say? That's heavy stuff."

"So is an automatic weapon."

Saul leaned against the wall. His face was thoughtful. "You're thinking what?"

"How many automatic weapons around?"

Saul smiled through his beard. "Ask the NRA, although even if they knew, they wouldn't tell you. So?"

"Oh, hell," Johnny said. "It looks like the organized thing, no? FBI man poking around, gunned down by a squirt gun, the body dropped from an aircraft, probably at night, in the middle of nowhere. With any luck, in two, three days the vultures and ravens and skunks would have made him hard, if not impossible, to identify. But three hikers found him first." He was silent, examining a new thought. "Anything about his clothes?"

"Like what?"

"Maybe a tear? From going through, or over, a chain-link fence?"

Saul shook his bearded head. "Nothing I saw."

"Then there isn't anything." Johnny nodded. Saul was nothing if not thorough. "Anything on his shoes? Dirt? Grass stains?"

"He'd been walking on pavement. Nothing there." Saul smiled again, suddenly. "I don't think even you could pick up tracks on dry pavement."

10

"I wouldn't even try. Where was he shot, front or back?"

"Front. Not too close, but not too far away, either. Light slugs. They deflect easily, so you don't want to be too far away when you start the action."

"Much blood wherever it was?"

Saul shook his head. "Only inside. Those slugs tear you up, but they don't usually come out."

A blank slate, Johnny was thinking, and yet there was something running around in the back of his mind. "Anything about the body?"

"Like what?"

"I don't know, and that's a fact."

"He was left-handed," Saul said. "But what does that prove?"

Johnny closed his eyes. He opened them again and shook his head. "No, he wasn't. Not in my office. I would have noticed. And not—yes, his shoulder holster was under his left arm. He was right-handed. He had to be. Why do you think not?"

Saul was frowning now. "He wore his watch on his right wrist like left-handers do. Digital watch with buttons to push."

Johnny closed his eyes again and was silent for long moments. He opened his eyes. "Anything on his wrist the watch was covering? A scar, maybe?"

"Yes, there's a scar, a small one, nothing disfiguring that he'd want to hide, just a scar like maybe an old burn, a little one." Saul was all interest now. "You seeing visions again? Your swami act?"

Johnny said slowly, "Could it be a scar made by removing something? Like maybe a tattoo?"

"Oh, my God," Saul said, "if you aren't the damnedest!"

"Just a guess," Johnny said. "It's far out."

"We'll see," Saul said. "We will sure as hell see."

That night, relaxed with Cassie on the sofa in front of a piñon fire, the dog Chico at their feet, "So that's where we stand," Johnny said. He glanced at Cassie's face, and one of his rare smiles appeared out of pure pleasure at the sight.

Cassie, Cassandra Enright, Ph.D., anthropologist, was slim and lovely, with even, friendly features and café-au-lait skin. "I'm a black chick," she had said once, "with a go-go dancer's carcass and a head stuffed to the eyeballs with anthropological erudition, and where do I find a man to go with all that?"

Her question had long since been answered by the man sitting beside her now. And there was the wonder, that the two of them, misfits both, had somehow miraculously and ecstatically come together. There were even times these days when Cassie was tempted to believe that there might be a humane and understanding God after all.

"Any thoughts, *chica?*" Johnny said.

The question, Cassie knew, was partly but not wholly rhetorical. Johnny, of all people, needed no one to tell him how to run his investigations; his record showed that. And yet, happily, there *was* a role that she could, and did, play—that of catalyst, sometimes asking questions that opened new avenues of thought, sometimes hearing a theory of his stated and, without even commenting upon it, realizing that it bounced back to him in some way altered. This was warm knowledge.

Now, "The way you spoke of him," she said, "seemed to indicate that you think Leon Bascomb is somehow involved, no?"

Johnny looked at her again. In the changing light cast by the fire, the harsh Indian lines of his face were emphasized. "And you don't?" he said.

"He is such a nice man," Cassie said, and smiled fondly. "That is pure feminine reaction. Since he has come on the museum board, I've gotten to know him better."

"I didn't know he *was* on your board," Johnny said.

Cassie smiled again. "Until now it didn't really seem worth mentioning. Museums are not your thing."

"Whatever concerns you concerns me," Johnny said. "You know that."

She did, and treasured the knowledge. She said nothing.

"So, what kind of guy is he?"

Cassie thought about it. "Polite, kind, considerate," she said at last, "and above all willing to listen. He admits his lack of technical knowledge. Not many successful people do. They think that because they succeeded at one thing, they have all the answers. Leon doesn't."

"Leon," Johnny said, and by the single word asked a question.

"He prefers it. He doesn't like to be called Mr. Bascomb."

All at once Johnny was thinking of something Higgins had said that day in his office. "Maybe," he said, "because that isn't his name."

"Johnny!"

Johnny's smile was sheepish. "Just thinking, *chica,*" he said. "Maybe seeing shadows and reflections the way Tony says I do. Let's call it a night and go to bed."

"That," Cassie said, "is the best offer I've had today."

Just before sleep came that night, Cassie said in a quiet, puzzled voice, "Did you mean what you said, that Bascomb isn't Leon's real name?"

"I don't know," Johnny said. "But it's something I'm going to find out."

2

Wallace was no help at all. "If Bascomb isn't his real name," he said on the telephone, "then I don't have any idea what is. All I know about him is that he was a prominent businessman in Miami."

"And you aren't interested in why he moved out here?" Johnny said. "Higgins said you were."

There was a hint of exasperation in Wallace's voice now. "Strictly between us," he said, "Higgins was sometimes a pain in the ass. He got ideas, or dreamed them up, and nothing could shake him out of them. He could be, like they say, a loose gun in a heavy sea." He paused. "But he was one of our people, so we *are* damned interested in finding out what happened to him, and who did it, and why. It's your jurisdiction, yes, but I'll expect you to keep me up to date."

"Will do," Johnny said, and hung up to lean back in his chair and stare at his thoughts.

Tony Lopez appeared in the doorway, had one look at Johnny's face, and turned away. To the sergeant at the front desk he said, "He's dreaming again," and shook his head slowly. To Tony, pure Hispanic, the

Indian side of Johnny smacked of drums and war chants and visions conjured up out of the smoke of lonely campfires while coyotes sang accompaniment in the darkness beyond.

Johnny came out of his office. "I'll be over in the Federal Building with Mark Hawley," he said, and walked out to his pickup.

Congressman Mark Hawley was not alone, but his longtime secretary told Johnny it was okay to go in. "He and Ben Hart are sipping whisky and swapping tall tales," she said, "and they'll be glad to see you."

They were. The congressman was in shirtsleeves, necktie loosened, at ease with a glass at hand and a bottle of the fine, smooth bourbon he kept sitting on his desk. Ben Hart wore his usual costume of worn, heeled boots, jeans, and a flannel shirt, the sleeves turned back on his brawny forearms. His hat was upside down on the congressman's desk, and his forehead above the hat line showed pink against the deep tan of the rest of his face.

"Set, son," the congressman said. "A drink? No? Well, each to his own taste. How's that wonderful female of yours? You know, you're a lucky man. If I were thirty, thirty-five years younger, I'd give you a run for your money in her direction, and that's a sure-God fact."

Ben Hart said, "You'd have me to buck, too." He studied Johnny's face. "Man's got something on his mind," he said.

Johnny nodded as he sat down. "A dead FBI man," he said, "and a man who calls himself Leon Bascomb." He looked from one to the other. "Ring any bells?"

Mark Hawley set down his glass of whisky. "'Calls himself,'" he said. "That means what?"

"I'm trying to find out. The dead FBI man said it wasn't his name." Johnny's voice was expressionless.

"I think you'd better begin at the beginning, son," the congressman said, and Ben Hart nodded agreement.

They listened in silence while Johnny recounted the tale. When he was done, Mark Hawley refilled his own and Ben Hart's glasses and leaned back in his chair again, his face contemplative. "And what do you want me to do, see what I can find out through Immigration, Miami court records, that kind of thing?"

"Just a hunch," Johnny said.

"Man's hunches," Ben Hart said, "usually play out pretty good."

"I'm aware of that," the congressman said. He was still looking at Johnny. "What else can you tell us, son?"

It was then that the phone on the desk buzzed. Mark Hawley picked it up, listened, and held it out to Johnny. "For you."

It was Saul Pentland, and his voice held mildly annoyed incredulity. "I think you have second sight," he said. "With ultraviolet light, and a couple of other little tricks we have, we brought up the reason for the scar on the dead man's wrist. It *was* a tattoo that had been removed. A snake, near as we could make out. So, what does that tell you?"

"I haven't the vaguest idea," Johnny said. Simple truth.

"But you'll find out," Saul said, merely stating a fact, "and when you do, let me know, huh?"

"Agreed. Thanks, Saul." Johnny hung up.

"Care to tell us?" the congressman said.

Johnny did, and when he was finished, the office was still.

Ben Hart said at last, "I never understood why a man gets his hide branded. We do it to cattle so we can tell whose is which, but—"

Mark Hawley said, "Some men do it for the same reason. That's what you're thinking, son? A kind of identification, like those numbers they tattooed in concentration camps, that kind of thing?"

"A possibility," Johnny said.

The congressman held his whisky glass up so he could admire the color of the liquor. "Son," he said, "maybe I'd best try to find out just how much the Bureau really knows about your dead agent Higgins. They pride themselves on their background checks, but so did British Intelligence, and a man named Kim Philby fooled *them* for years." He lowered the glass and looked at Johnny. "What you've got here, son, is a can of worms."

"Or a ball of snakes," Ben Hart said, "like when rattlers hole up together for the winter." He paused. "You going to tell this to that fellow Wallace, Higgins's boss?"

Johnny looked at Mark Hawley.

"I'd say," the congressman said, "just let it lay while I see what I can maybe turn up. No need to get Wallace in an uproar—yet."

"My thinking, too," Johnny said.

"So, what's next?" This was Ben Hart again.

"Why," Johnny said, "I think I'd like to meet Leon Bascomb himself."

Ben Hart tossed down his whisky, heaved himself up from his chair, and picked up his hat. "Good idea. Suppose I go along, just for company? Mark and me, we drank his liquor and ate his fancy food. I'll pay him a thank-you call. Man can't object to that, now, can he?"

The main gate to the Bascomb property was closed, and a man stepped out of the small building beyond it to look questioningly at Johnny's pickup.

"Same feller checked invitations," Ben Hart said. "They didn't fancy party crashers. Looks like they don't fancy visitors, either."

"We'll see," Johnny said. He got out of the truck and walked up to the gate. To the man, he said, "Santo Cristo police." He showed his ID. "I'd like to have a talk with Bascomb. My name is Ortiz."

"I'll check," the man said, and stepped back into the small building. In a few moments the gate swung open and the man appeared and waved them through. The gate, Johnny noticed in the mirror, closed again immediately.

"Careful feller, isn't he?" Ben said. "Me, all I've got is a cattle guard."

"And eight miles of road to your ranch house," Johnny said, showing one of his rare smiles. "Plenty of time for a man to decide if he really wants to go the distance." He glanced at Ben's face.

"No reason a man shouldn't," Ben said. "I'm friendly. Most times, that is."

And other times, Johnny thought, remembering other occasions, the old man could be as dangerous as a grizzly bear.

A man in a white jacket waited at the front door of the big house. Hispanic, Johnny decided, and said in Spanish, "We wish to see the Señor Bascomb."

"This way," the man said, also in Spanish, and led them down a hallway to a large, book-lined study, where Bascomb waited.

He wore one of his monogrammed, short-sleeved shirts, tailored trousers, and tasseled loafers. "Gentlemen," he said. "Mr. Hart, isn't it? A pleasure to see you again, sir. And Lieutenant Ortiz?" He smiled. "Oh, yes, I have heard quite a bit about you, Lieutenant, from the charming Dr. Enright, among others. What can I do for you?"

"A man named Higgins," Johnny said, "Walter Higgins. Does the name mean anything to you?"

Bascomb thought for a moment and then, still smiling, shook his head. "I don't believe I know anyone by that name, Lieutenant. Should I?"

"Just a guess," Johnny said. "He is, was, an FBI man. He was interested in you, so I thought perhaps you might have met him."

"'Was an FBI man'?" Bascomb said.

"He's dead. Somebody pumped some bullets into him and then dropped him over on Elk Ridge from an aircraft."

Bascomb's smile was gone now. "I don't think I understand, Lieutenant. Are you thinking that I have any connection?"

"Like I said, just a guess."

"I am afraid a very bad one, then." Bascomb was silent, thoughtful for a few moments. "You said he was interested in me? May I ask why?"

"He wondered why you had moved here from Miami."

"If he had asked me, Lieutenant, I would have told him. Miami's climate is not all that pleasant all year. I find this far more agreeable."

"I thought it might be something like that."

Again Bascomb was silent for a few moments, frowning now. He said at last, "I am not sure I like this, Lieutenant. I am trying to be agreeable, but,

20

frankly, I must say that I resent the implication you seem to be making. I did not know anyone named Walter Higgins, and I certainly had nothing at all to do with his death. I am a businessman, not some kind of mobster as you seem to think."

"Like I said, just a guess." Johnny looked around at the shelves of books, the gleaming paneling. "Nice place you have."

"Is that supposed to mean something sinister, too, Lieutenant?"

"Just an observation."

"You gave a good party," Ben Hart said. "Good liquor, good food, nice folks."

"I am trying to fit into the community," Bascomb said.

"Then I'd say you're doing it the right way," Johnny said. "Thanks for your time. Sorry my guesses were bad. Sorry they bothered you."

"Do you know, Lieutenant," Bascomb said, "I am not sure that you are. I am not sure what you really had in mind, either, but I don't think I like it."

"Sorry about that, too," Johnny said. "Let's go, Ben, and stop bothering the man."

Ben waited until they were back in the pickup and through the gate before he made his first comment. Then, "You sort of put the spurs to him, boy. Trying to make him buck?"

"Just throwing a rock into the bushes," Johnny said, "to see what might come out."

Ben nodded understandingly. "That's one way to stir up game. Sometimes it works, sometimes it doesn't. Sometimes all it does it scare the game away."

"I don't think he'll run," Johnny said. "Whatever his reasons were for moving from Miami, he's got too much invested here."

They drove in silence for a little time before Johnny said suddenly, "How's for a ride in your chopper?" Ben had long ago decided that a helicopter was the best way for him to cover his 65,000 acres of ranch.

"What do you have in mind?"

"A look-see at the place on Elk Ridge where we found Higgins. Just a feeling."

Ben nodded. "We'll do her. Hunches are good things to follow."

From 12,000 feet, the world below seemed to stand on end. It was late summer, but on the north slopes of the higher Sangre de Cristo peaks snow still lingered and might hold until fresh snow began to fall in late September or October.

The deep Pecos Valley showed green, and the river at its bottom romped and roiled, here leaving a small, quiet pool, there showing white water over rocks and shallows. You could almost hear the water singing as it ran its joyous course, Johnny thought, and did not say aloud.

He pointed ahead toward Elk Ridge. "That talus slope," he said. "Near that Bristlecone pine, see?"

"You've got it," Ben said, and altered course. "You want to go lower? We'll bounce around some, but that makes me no never-mind."

Johnny shook his head. "This is fine. We've got the broad view."

Ben glanced sideways. "You know what you're looking for?"

"No."

"Thought not. So let's just circle around and see what we can see."

There was not much beyond the towering Ponderosa pines, the lower brush and scrub oak, and the foot-trail, from above plain as could be, winding in and among the greenery, with here and there bare rocky outcroppings with their trailing talus slopes.

Ben said suddenly, "There! Bear! See him?"

"Her," Johnny said. "And she's already sent her cubs up that dead tree." He watched the bear quietly. "She isn't sure about us," he said. There was warmth and understanding in his tone.

"But if we landed," Ben said, "she'd take us on without even a second thought. She'd take anything on to protect those cubs."

Johnny nodded silently. All things were arranged, he was thinking, each creature in its way predictable and in its right and proper place—all except man, who sometimes turned rogue without reason or warning.

He said suddenly, "A weasel in a henhouse," and glanced at Ben to see if he understood.

"In a killing rage?" Ben said. "That what you mean?"

"Exactly. Why go to all the trouble to fly Higgins up here and drop him? He was already dead, and there are 10,000 square miles of countryside down below where they could have dumped him."

"So you tell me," Ben said. "A man would have to hate awful hard to go about it that way."

"Bueno," Johnny said. "So now we think we maybe know why—but what was behind it?"

Ben said, "I can usually figure out what a horse has in mind before he does it, but folks are sometimes way beyond me. That's your briar patch."

"And right now," Johnny said, "about all I can see in it are brambles."

3

Santo Cristo is an ancient city, wearing its age with subdued, rather graceful pride, and coping fairly easily with its mixture of Indian, Hispanic, and Anglo cultures, mores, and histories.

In 1540 Francisco Vásquez de Coronado came through leading an expedition up from Mexico City; went as far east as what is now Kansas in search of reported gold and wealth, decided that his Indian guides had been lying to him—as they had—had them strangled, and returned to Mexico City.

It was not until 1610, 70 years later, that Juan de Oñate, also from Mexico City, formally established Santo Cristo as a Spanish capital of the New World.

In many ways, despite its considerable sophistication, the city retains small-town characteristics, one of which being that information and rumors concerning persons and events of interest spread rapidly.

Johnny went to see Bert Clancy, president of the Santo Cristo unit of the fourteen-state-bank network. Bert was a genial type, well known and well thought of in Santo Cristo and throughout the Southwest. He was large and rumpled, and wore heeled boots with his dark suit. A Fort Worth-style Stetson hung on the coatrack in the corner.

"What brings you here?" Bert said as he shook Johnny's hand and indicated a visitor's chair.

"Leon Bascomb," Johnny said, and watched a wary look come into Bert's eyes, the look of a poker player who watches an opponent draw only one card.

Bert sat down behind his desk. "What about him?"

"Well-heeled," Johnny said. "There doesn't seem to be much doubt about that."

"Well off," Bert said cautiously, "I'd say that. Not really big rich like some Texans I know." He paused and studied Johnny's face, an exercise in futility, as he knew well. "Why? What's your interest in him?"

"Just curious," Johnny said. "I get that way sometimes."

Bert decided on silence. Banker's reticence sometimes came in handy.

"I understand," Johnny said, "that he's been in real estate. Miami? Here, too? Aside from his house, I mean?"

Bert relaxed a trifle. "It's no secret that he's invested in the new Plaza Building. Anything wrong with that?"

"You've got me wrong," Johnny said. "I don't know a thing against the man." He accented the verb slightly. "Stocks, too? Bonds?"

"I believe he has a portfolio, yes. Most men in his position do."

"Anything else you know about?"

Bert took a deep breath. "I've never known you to ask questions without you had reasons," he said.

Johnny nodded affably. "And I've never known you to clam up unless you had something on your mind, Bert. You want I should go poking around in other directions? I'm just trying to get to know something about the man." Johnny was silent for a few moments, seemingly hesitant. "He's on the museum board," he said at last, "Cassie's museum board."

"Oh," Bert said, and smiled happily. "It's a personal thing then. That's different."

Johnny waited in silence with that bone-bred patience of his.

"The thing is," Bert said, "we're, ah, thinking of asking him to join our board, too. So if there's anything about the fellow we ought to know . . . ?" He left the question unfinished.

"Nothing I know of," Johnny said.

"We've checked him out, of course," Bert said. "Even got in touch with some folks in Miami." He shook his head. "Clean as a hound's tooth, near as we can make out, else we wouldn't even be considering asking him to come on the board."

"Of course not," Johnny said.

"Like I said," Bert said, "it's no secret he's into real estate, the Plaza Building. And he has a piece of the Cadillac dealership, and some of Todd Van and Storage, they're associated nationally with International, you know, and Bascomb was asking me what I thought of the new industrial park some of the local boys are trying to set up to pull in high-tech industry. That kind of thing." Bert spread his hands. "I'd say he's an all-right fellow, Johnny, and that's a fact, an addition to Santo Cristo."

Johnny got up. "Thanks, Bert," he said. "You've made me feel a lot better."

"Glad to help," Bert said. "Anytime."

Johnny walked out of the bank and over to the Plaza, where he sat down on one of the benches, looked without seeing at the hordes of *turistas* strolling aimlessly, and thought about what Bert had told him. He reached no conclusions.

Leon Bascomb, wearing another of his monogrammed short-sleeved shirts, tailored poplin trousers, and tasseled loafers, sat in his book-lined study and spoke in fluent, unaccented Spanish with the man named Jorge Trujillo, a Cuban via Miami, for several years now a Santo Cristo resident. Jorge Trujillo was uneasy.

"Obviously," Bascomb said, "they have found the body and identified it. You stripped him of all identification first?"

"Everything. I left not even a handkerchief."

Bascomb was silent for a few moments, thinking hard. "Then he left a trail," he said at last, "else they would not have been able to identify him so quickly. Whom did he see before he came here?"

Jorge shook his head. "I do not know."

"Then find out. But without attracting attention, understood?"

"*Sí.*"

Again Bascomb was silent for a time. Then, "Elk Ridge, the policeman said. Where is that?"

"It is the ridge behind the big mountains of the Sangre de Cristo range."

"And why did you choose that place?"

Jorge spread his hands. "It is lonely. Except in hunting season, no one goes there."

"Someone did."

"Hikers." Jorge shrugged. "They go everywhere." He hesitated. "You wanted the body dropped from altitude. I wished to attract no attention, and Elk Ridge is a lonely place."

"There are many lonely places in this God-

27

abandoned country. There is that big ranch west of town, for example."

Jorge's face turned solemn and he shook his head slowly. "The ranch of Señor Hart? No. That is a place to stay away from."

"Why?"

"Because of Señor Hart himself."

"That old man?"

Jorge nodded. *"Sí.* He is called *el oso pardo,* the grizzly bear." Jorge smiled, a blend of apology, grudging admiration, and definite conviction. "When cattle are stolen, or mutilated, as has happened since I have lived here, none of these things have happened on the ranch of Señor Hart. It is well known that it is not safe to molest him."

Bascomb looked doubtful, but said nothing.

Jorge said, "Had you merely wanted the body disposed of, I could have taken it by car to some lonely arroyo where only the vultures and the coyotes and ravens would have found it quickly. But you wanted it dropped from altitude." He spread his hands, and his face took on a mine-not-to-question-why expression.

Nothing changed in Bascomb's face. *"Bueno,"* he said. "It is done now. It remains only for you to find out whom he saw before he came here."

"Could he not have told his own people in the Bureau where he was going, and why?"

"No." Bascomb's voice was definite. "If he had, it would not have been the local policeman who came here. It would have been the FBI itself. I know how they work." He sat up straight and made a quick, peremptory gesture. "Enough. See what you can find out. Understood?"

"Sí."

"And without attracting attention."

"Understood."

Johnny drove his pickup 65 miles and 2,000 feet of elevation down to the city, something he did as infrequently as possible. The city, with about eight times the population of Santo Cristo, had, in Johnny's estimation, long since lost whatever character it had to become merely one more faceless American population center of a trifle less than half a million people.

He asked to see, and was shown in to, the federal magistrate Higgins had agreed was a hard-nosed son of a bitch. The magistrate's name was Gus Goddard.

"Sit down, Lieutenant," Goddard said. "What brings you here?"

"FBI man Walter Higgins, the late Walter Higgins."

The magistrate was still addicted to cigarettes. He lit one now and blew out a cloud of smoke. "I read about that," he said. "The story was lurid. Was it also true—that he had been shot, killed, and *then* dropped from an aircraft on a lonely mountain ridge?"

"All true," Johnny said, and hesitated before adding, "Your Honor."

"I leave the title in the courtroom," Goddard said, and blew more smoke thoughtfully. "Do you know why? Why he was killed, and why they, whoever they were, then went to the trouble of flying the body into the mountains and dropping it there?"

"Only a guess," Johnny said. "Somebody hated him bad, or—" He paused to study a new thought. "—it was meant to be an example to others."

Goddard thought about it, and nodded slowly. "I see your point. But where do I come in?"

"Apparently you told him to touch base with me."

"I did. He was going into your jurisdiction and I thought you ought to know about it."

"For that," Johnny said, and smiled briefly, *"gracias."*

"De nada." The words came out easily, and without accent.

"Did he tell you, or give you any idea why he was coming up to Santo Cristo?" Johnny said.

Goddard dropped ashes into the ashtray and shook his head. "He was . . . evasive. I gathered it was something of a fishing expedition he had in mind—which was one of the reasons I told him to check with you. With an FBI badge to show, some agents tend to poke into matters and ask sometimes embarrassing questions about things that are none of their business."

"What I don't understand," Johnny said, "is why he came to you in the first place."

Goddard smiled. "He wanted a warrant, a John Doe search warrant. I told him I'd think about it—*after* I saw some facts, some kind of probable cause. He was not happy."

Johnny smiled again. "He called you a hard-nosed son of a bitch," he said.

"Did he, now?" Goddard, too, was smiling. "I am flattered, Lieutenant, I purely am." He was silent for a moment. "The newspaper account did not mention the specific location where the body was found," he said.

"Elk Ridge. It's—"

"I know it well," Goddard said. "I've hunted there. Lovely views in all directions. Frankly, I hoped I wouldn't find a deer, and I didn't. I just enjoyed the walk in the solitude."

The man had to be Western-born and -bred, Johnny

thought. Aloud, "I know exactly what you mean," he said. And then he went back to the main point. "Did he mention a name to you?"

"What name, Lieutenant?"

"Leon Bascomb."

Goddard shook his head, had one more puff, and ground out the cigarette in the ashtray. "He did not mention that name," he said. "And it means nothing to me."

Johnny stood up. "I was afraid of that." He held out his hand. "Thanks for your time—Judge."

"Most folks call me Gus—if they use a name, that is, and not an epithet." His handshake was firm.

"Johnny," Johnny said, and for the third time showed a smile. "Unless the same thing applies about the epithet."

He walked out to his car no further along than he had been, but feeling good anyway. There was something about meeting a man you could like immediately, as he had the magistrate.

It had not always been so, he thought as he got into the truck; before Cassie's softening influence, all men had been, if not enemies, at least persons to be viewed with wariness. Especially Anglos. The miracle was Cassie, and the changes she had wrought, and for all that he had no words, only continual warm astonishment.

It was early the next week when Leon Bascomb invited Cassie to lunch at the Palace. "All open and aboveboard," he told her in that polite, friendly way of his. "I am a neophyte and you are the expert, and I think there are broad matters concerning the museum and its aims that you could explain to me. If you would take the time, that is?"

"How," Cassie asked Johnny that night, "could I turn down a request like that?"

"No way, *chica*," Johnny said. "The man may actually be exactly what he seems."

"But you don't think so."

"I'm trying to keep an open mind. Enjoy your lunch."

Bascomb was already waiting in a booth when Cassie came into the restaurant. He stood up, smiling, and shook her hand. "Thank you for coming," he said.

Cassie was not sure what she had been expecting, but she would have been less than honest with herself if she had not admitted that Johnny's suspicions about the man had influenced her. All during lunch she searched for hidden meanings behind his questions and his conversation, and found nothing at all. She did not know whether to be relieved or disappointed.

To begin with, over glasses of white wine, "The museums here," Bascomb said, "seem to exert a greater influence on the entire community than I have ever encountered elsewhere. Why is that, do you think?"

Cassie had never thought about it in exactly that way, but the answer came easily enough. "Maybe it's because the past *is* so much of Santo Cristo." When she smiled, her face was alight with beauty. "It is one of the city's principal charms. That, and the fact that the three cultures, Indian, Hispanic, and Anglo, live in real harmony. Through the museums we try to see how that is possible."

"Pots," Bascomb said, "and rugs and sand paintings?"

"And artwork, both ancient and contemporary, and tribal memories along with old-world and Latin American Hispanic traditions together with our own, all blended to produce the society we have here today."

Bascomb said, "Your friend Lieutenant Ortiz?"

Cassie decided the question was innocent. "He's a mixture of all three cultures—Indian, Hispanic, and Anglo."

"And you? You came here, as I did. You are not native."

Cassie smiled. Once upon a time, she thought, she might not have been able to. "I'm an Anglo," she said. "I'm black, but because I'm neither Indian nor Hispanic, I'm Anglo. There are only those three categories here." She smiled again. "A friend of mine here, a weaver, is obviously of Oriental background, but she is an Anglo, too. For the same reason. Confusing, isn't it?"

"It does simplify things," Bascomb said. "Another glass of wine?"

And so the luncheon went, Cassie told Johnny later, pleasant enough, but also innocent, even innocuous, and seemingly without point.

"Chica," Johnny said, his voice soft with affection, "just having lunch with a female as attractive as you is definitely not pointless. It is very appealing to the male ego."

Cassie's smile was automatic, acknowledging the compliment, but her face was thoughtful. "He did say one thing," she said, "or, rather, ask it, that I found odd." Her smile now was almost embarrassed. "He asked if I was an only child."

Johnny thought about it. "You told him yes. And?"

"And when I asked him why he had asked," Cassie said, "he said it was because he had always found only children somehow special."

"Was that all?"

"No. I asked him if he was an only child, too. I thought it was almost obligatory to ask."

Johnny waited in patient silence.

"He said no," Cassie said. "He said he had had a brother once, but that he had died."

"Only that?"

Cassie nodded. "But I thought the whole exchange odd, don't you?"

"Out of the ordinary, yes," Johnny said, and that was all.

4

Johnny had a caller the next morning. Her name was Mollie Smith, and she reminded Johnny of a desert pocket mouse, small and quick in her movements and perpetually fearful outside her protective cholla cactus nest, all alone in the big world.

"My real name," she said, "is Mary, of course, but I've always been called Mollie." Even her tone seemed wary, as if, challenged, she would not hesitate to retract whatever she had said, and probably flee. "And Smith is my maiden name. I've used it for the last year and more."

"I see," Johnny said, and didn't. He waited for explanation.

"My real, legal name is Higgins. I am, or I guess I was, Walter's wife." She was silent for a little time, and Johnny hoped she was not going to cry. " 'Next of kin,' " she said presently. "Isn't that a dreadful phrase?"

Johnny agreed that it did not strike a sympathetic note. "What can I do for you, Mrs. Higgins?" he said.

Mollie drew a deep breath. "The Bureau notified me, of course," she said, and seemed to wait for

Johnny's approving nod of understanding before she felt it safe to go on. "I mean, Walter's apartment down in the city, his things, and all—they're mine now. The Bureau said so." Again she waited until Johnny, by nodding, seemed to give her encouragement. "But," she said then, "Walter's . . . personal things that he carried with him . . ." She stopped in pure helplessness and just sat, her eyes on Johnny's face.

"We have none, Mrs. Higgins," Johnny said gently. "Nothing beyond the clothes he was wearing." He paused. "And his empty holster."

Mollie blinked. "No wallet?" she said. "No keys? No—nothing?"

"Nothing. I am sorry."

Mollie Higgins blinked again. "Oh, dear," she said, nothing more.

Johnny said carefully, "Was there something, Mrs. Higgins, something—special, out of the ordinary, that you would have expected to find?"

"No. Nothing like that."

"A moment," Johnny said, suddenly remembering. "I was wrong. We do have his wristwatch." Which he wore on the wrong wrist, presumably in order to cover an old scar—why?

Mollie's face brightened perceptibly. "I gave it to him," she said.

"I'm sure you may have it," Johnny said. "I'll make the arrangements." He picked up a pencil. "Where should we have it sent?" He wrote down the address of the apartment down in the city, and nodded.

"Thank you, Lieutenant." Mollie had risen. "Thank you very much."

"Not at all." Johnny watched her—*scurry* was the word that came to mind as she made her quick way

36

down the hall and outside. And when the door had closed after her, he picked up the phone and called Saul Pentland at the state police lab. "Higgins's wristwatch," he said to Saul.

"What about it?"

Johnny's voice was expressionless. "I don't know. Have it checked, will you? Is there anything special about it?"

"Like what?"

"Como dije, like I said, I don't know." Then, "Wait a moment." It had been a gift, Mollie had said. "Is there an inscription, maybe a date or something?"

"Tell me, *amigo,"* Saul said in his patient bearded-prophet's voice, "do you know what you are after?"

"I do not," Johnny said, "and that is a fact." He hung up slowly and leaned back in his chair to think. He roused himself at last and placed a call to Wallace, the FBI man down in the city. To him he explained about Mollie Smith Higgins.

"His wife," Wallace said, "yes. They were separated, but not divorced, so technically she is next of kin and entitled. Why?"

Johnny produced a faint smile. "I'm getting tired of saying I don't know. But I don't." Tony Lopez would have been able to explain that the Indian was seeing visions again—and there was nothing to be done about it. "So, thanks," Johnny said. "Anything turns up, I'll be in touch."

"She's a funny one," Wallace said unexpectedly. "Afraid of her own shadow." Pause. "Apparently."

Johnny's eyebrows rose. "Oh?" he said. "Apparently?"

"Off the record," Wallace said after a short, contemplative pause, "she had a break-in a year or so back. It was nighttime and she was alone." He paused again. "She had a little .25 automatic Higgins had given her, one of those Banker's Specials, you know?"

"I do." Johnny was all attention now. "What happened?"

"Six rounds," Wallace said. "She put all six in the intruder's belly. The ambulance guys took him away in a body bag."

Johnny hung up and stared thoughtfully at the wall for a long time. Obviously, he was thinking, there was more to little Mollie Smith Higgins, who reminded him of a fearful desert pocket mouse, than her appearance would tend to suggest. Interesting.

Leon Bascomb parked the gray Cadillac in one of the municipal parking lots and went on foot to the cathedral. It had the look of age, he thought, but he had known others far older. No matter. It would serve.

He went into the cool darkness beyond the huge, carved doors, knelt, crossed himself, rose, and walked steadily up the aisle toward the altar. There he knelt again, and again crossed himself, and, eyes closed, spoke silently a prayer—not for himself, but for the soul of the man who once had been his brother.

Rising, he walked back down the aisle, paused at the doorway to turn and genuflect a third time, and then walked out into the brilliance of the day. He felt better, easier in his mind.

He was not basically a devout man; in fact, religion had come late into his life, only after his mother, divorced, had married Bascomb, who was originally from Cuba and brought up in the faith. But for Leon Bascomb, the adopted son, the Church with its promises of inner peace was occasionally a direction in which to turn in time of trouble, doubt, or uncertainty. As now.

He disliked the appearance of Higgins, the FBI man. He disliked the appearance so soon after Higgins's demise of the Hispanic-Indian-Anglo cop, Johnny Ortiz, who had a look in his eye that made a man want to look over his shoulder. Nothing, as far as Bascomb could determine, was amiss. And yet he had a feeling that would not be denied, and he had long ago learned that it paid to heed such feelings.

He walked back to his car, ignoring the *turistas* who seemed to be everywhere. Some of the females among them were young, to his objective eye attractive, even in their braless, bouncing way somewhat provocative, he supposed; but females, as such, had never appealed to him. Women tended to make trouble, and he had always considered himself lucky that he found them unnecessary.

He paid his quarter at the parking lot and drove out to the Todd Van & Storage Company.

Joe Todd, Joseph Henry Todd, Jr., was in his office, and he greeted Bascomb with a mixture of friendly deference and faint unease. Without Bascomb's financial aid, Todd would have been in some difficulties, and he was not a man to question manna from heaven. Still . . . "What can I do for you?" he said, and smiled as he added facetiously, "You're not thinking of moving again already?"

Bascomb took a chair. "I like it here. I'll be around awhile." He, too, could smile, although if one looked carefully it was evident that his smile did not reach his eyes. "How's business?"

"Slow." Simple truth. "And pretty much all one way—*from* California. It used to be the Texans who had the cash. Now . . ." Todd shrugged.

"You need more connections in Texas, Louisiana," Bascomb said thoughtfully, "as a matter of fact, in a lot of places east of us. People are moving west in droves. There is business to be had."

"We're off the beaten trail," Todd said. "Van traffic goes through Albuquerque south of us, or Denver to the north. Santo Cristo is a detour."

Bascomb shook his head. He had given the matter careful thought. "Not that far. And if you offered part-load service and direct routes through all the small places scattered around Arizona, you could send your vans at a profit instead of near-empty on their way out to pick up that California business."

Todd looked doubtful. "I've thought of it, but—" He shook his head.

"But what?"

"It would mean dealing with all kinds of carriers instead of just the ones we're used to."

"So?" Bascomb's voice was still friendly. "I'm not one to make a loan and then tell a man how to run his business. On the other hand, if I can make suggestions that could benefit him, and me in the long run, I'd be less than intelligent if I didn't make them, don't you think?"

Todd smiled. "Obviously."

"I admire healthy balance sheets, especially when I have money involved," Bascomb said, and he, too, was smiling. "And I have connections here and there that just might fit in. Suppose I make a few inquiries?"

Todd sat silent, uncertain but under the circumstances almost helpless; with Bascomb's loan, he had already lost a measure of independence.

Bascomb stood up. "Think about it," he said. "In the meantime, I'll put out a few feelers, no commitments, and just see what I can come up with. Okay?"

"If you put it that way," Todd said, somewhat relieved.

"That's how it is," Bascomb said. "I'll be in touch."

The service down in the city for Walter Higgins was sparsely attended. Mollie Smith Higgins was there, of course, along with Wallace and a few of the FBI staff, but that was all.

And when the short service ended, Wallace walked out to his car with the widow. "I don't want to intrude," he said, "but we'll be glad to take care of the ashes if you would like us to."

Mollie Higgins smiled in her tentative, shy way. "I would like that very much," she said. "Walter and I . . ."

"I quite understand."

"You are very kind."

"The least we can do." Wallace was silent for a few paces. Then, "You are going back East again?"

"No." Even the single word seemed hedged with apprehension. "I think I like it here." She smiled quickly. "Don't you think Santo Cristo is lovely?"

"I do," Wallace said, "although I don't get there much. Our work is mostly down here." He hesitated. "But jobs up there, I understand, are not easy to find."

Mollie Higgins said as if she were explaining a sacred secret, "I was thinking of the Scientific Lab." She looked shyly up at Wallace's face as if asking his permission.

Wallace opened his mouth and closed it again silently. He said at last, "Come to think of it, Mrs. Higgins, I don't even know what you—I mean—"

"What my skills are?"

"Exactly."

Mollie Higgins seemed embarrassed. She said in a

very small voice, "I have a Ph.D. in mathematics. Computers are my specialty."

"You could," Wallace told Johnny on the phone later, "have knocked me over with a feather. I never thought she was exactly stupid, but mathematics? And computers?"

"As you pointed out," Johnny said, "she is not run-of-the-mill, is she?"

"Reason I called," Wallace said, "is, well, her husband *was* one of ours and we feel a certain— responsibility for her as his widow. If you could see any way to give her a hand?"

"I'll see what I can do," Johnny said. "She— interests me."

And so it was through Johnny that Mollie Smith Higgins met Lucille and Waldo Harrington, world-class physicists up at the Scientific Lab. "She," Johnny told Lucille, whom he had first met when her son was murdered, "comes on like a mouse, a desert pocket mouse. Do you know them?" Lucille did not. "They make their homes in jumping cholla," Johnny said, "and there is no more vicious cactus in existence. Inside a jumping cholla, pocket mice can thumb their noses at coyotes, foxes, badgers, hawks, anything except maybe a snake. Outside their cholla they are frightened of anything that moves."

Lucille had a quiet laugh. "And what is Mrs. Higgins's sheltering cholla?" she said.

"I don't know yet," Johnny said. And then, in a wild leap of imagination, "Maybe it's her brains." He was silent a moment, thinking of the story of the intruder taken away in a body bag. "And a basic—I guess *courage* is the word. I'll tell you that story sometime."

"I will be happy to meet her," Lucille Harrington said. "We just might be able to find a place for her."

Mollie Higgins came to see Johnny after meeting Lucille Harrington. "I wanted to thank you," she said.

"De nada."

"She made me feel so—at home," Mollie said. "I had heard of her, of course, and of her husband. They are very important people in the scientific community."

Johnny produced one of his rare smiles.

"But you knew that, of course," Mollie said. "She, Mrs. Harrington, speaks very highly of you."

"I am flattered. I think very highly of her." In more ways than one; there were few persons, male or female, who were as high on Johnny's opinion list as Lucille Harrington. "Can she help you?"

For only a few moments the timid mask was set aside. "Thanks to her," Mollie said, "I have been interviewed at the lab, and I have been promised a job. After security checks, of course." Immediately she looked faintly embarrassed, as if she had been caught boasting.

"Congratulations," Johnny said, and opened his desk drawer. "Since I knew you were coming up," he said, "I had your husband's watch sent over here instead of down to the apartment." He held it out, and she took it with a grateful smile.

It was a fine watch, Johnny was thinking, a Seiko alarm-chronograph that would do just about everything but cook breakfast. It had probably cost Mollie a bundle. But, as nearly as Saul Pentland could tell, there was nothing about the watch, beyond a date inscribed on the back, that was at all out of the ordinary, and Johnny could only think that sentimentality was the single factor that could explain Mollie's obvious pleasure in having it now. But there was, of course, one more thing.

"Your husband," Johnny said, "wore the watch on his right wrist. But he was not left-handed. Why do you think he did that?"

Once again, only briefly, the timid mask was set aside. "Oh, no," Mollie said. "He always wore it on his left wrist." The mask was quickly back in place. "I am sorry," she said. "To contradict you, I mean."

"I was probably mistaken," Johnny said, and smiled again. "No problem. I frequently am."

He sat for a long time in thought after Mollie Higgins had left. Finally he called in Tony Lopez, who leaned comfortably against the wall to listen.

Johnny explained about the scar the watch had covered when Higgins was found. "But," he said, "she, his wife, says he always wore the watch on his other wrist. What do we make of that?"

Tony spread his hands, shrugged hugely, and showed white teeth in a broad smile. *"Amigo,* you tell me."

Something was scurrying around in Johnny's mind and he tried, and failed, to pin it down.

"Maybe just this once," Tony said thoughtfully, "he didn't want the scar seen? Maybe the rest of the time he didn't care?"

"Go into that." All at once Johnny's voice was sharp.

Tony shrugged again. "Everybody has scars. They're no big deal. Nobody notices them."

"But," Johnny said, "just one person might? One person might know how the scar came to be there, and why?" He nodded abruptly. *"Bueno.* Maybe not progress, but perhaps a faint beginning of understanding, no?"

"For you, maybe," Tony said. "But not for me." The *brujo,* witch, was seeing things in smoke again, he

44

thought, and that brought to mind a tale he had once heard about old Mark Hawley and Johnny.

"What beats me," the congressman had said, according to the tale, "is how we Anglos managed to go to the mat with your people and come out on top."

"Simple," Johnny had said. "You stole our sheep."

Maybe the Anglos had been able to do it, Tony thought now, but he personally wanted no kind of confrontation with Johnny—ever.

5

That night in front of a piñon fire, Cassie on the sofa beside him and Chico—Chico II, part collie, part husky, part shepherd, all New Mexican—at their feet, Johnny spoke of little Mollie Higgins.

"I've met her," Cassie said, and smiled at the look of surprise on Johnny's face. "She came to see me at the museum today, and we spent some time together. She is going to live here, she said, so she wants to know about Santo Cristo and its history. Is that so odd?"

"Most people," Johnny said, "live their lives here and all they know about the place is what they just happen to hear and maybe remember."

"Mollie," Cassie said, "is not most people. Haven't you seen that already?"

"Yes, ma'am." Johnny's smile was sheepish.

"She is not, as you think, a desert pocket mouse, Johnny. Look behind that timid act."

"And see the tiger?"

"No. See the person. As Lucille Harrington did."

"And as you have?"

46

Cassie's smile was gentle and fond. It lighted her face and her eyes and brought additional beauty into her smooth face. "Modesty aside, yes," she said. "Mollie and I are . . . on the same wavelength."

Charlie Cottrell, the local Cadillac dealer, admired Leon Bascomb's car. Charlie had dealt in automobiles all of his adult life, and recognized custom work when he saw it. "Maybe it's about time you brought it in for servicing?" he said, hoping to get a closer look.

Bascomb shook his head, smiling. "I have my own mechanic," he said. "He keeps this and the chopper in first-class shape." He made a deprecatory gesture. "Not that I'm running down your service department," he said. "You understand that."

"*Our* service department," Charlie said. "And, you'll be happy to hear, business is good. Booming. You don't need to worry about your investment."

"I don't tend to worry about things," Bascomb said. "If you plan them right, they work out."

It was the calm self-assurance of the man that Charlie had noticed before and found himself resenting because his own confidence in himself nowhere near approached the same standard. What he had, he had worked hard to obtain, and sometimes things had turned out well and sometimes there had been failures —experiences he had always assumed to be more or less universal. But he simply could not equate failure with Leon Bascomb, for whom everything always seemed to come up roses, and it was this that galled him.

"I was going to send you a detailed profit-and-loss statement," he said now somewhat stiffly, "but if you don't want to bother with it . . ." He shrugged.

Bascomb studied Charlie's face in appraising silence for a few moments. "I don't recall saying that," he said at last. "I said I did not tend to worry, which does not mean that I do not like to keep an eye on things. Understood?"

There was an arrogance in the man, too, Charlie was thinking, and he could resent that as well. But he produced his salesman's smile and his salesman's tone as he said, "Understood perfectly. You will have the statement soonest."

He watched Bascomb walk out to his gray Cadillac and get in. The heavy sound of the car door closing did not, to Charlie's experienced ear, sound quite normal, and he began to wonder about it. And then, for the first time, about Bascomb.

Congressman Mark Hawley, again home from Washington, summoned Johnny. "Set, son, and help yourself." He indicated the bottle of bourbon on his desk. His voice took on a musing, reminiscent note. "Used to be there were House members who appreciated good drinking liquor, but times have changed." He shook his head sadly. "A bunch of white wine drinkers now, or fancy mixed drinks like martinis." He poured himself another shot and sat up straight. "Now to business," he said. "Your man Walter Higgins. Still interested?"

"Very much so."

The congressman nodded. "Raised by his father, a cop, apparently a down-the-line Christer. Seems the boy, Walter, ran a trifle wild when he was young, and the old man found out about it and there was hell to pay. Threatened the boy with a reformatory, but never went that far. Instead he up and moved, taking the

48

boy with him, of course, away from one of those little towns around Miami clear out to Michigan."

Johnny's face was impassive, but his thoughts were running free. He sat silent, his drink untouched.

"Father," Mark Hawley said, "went to the only work he knew in Michigan, back on the police force again. Made sergeant. Exemplary record. Just how he straightened the boy out, nobody seems to know, maybe beat the daylights out of him. Anyway, Walter shaped up, graduated high in his high-school class, went to college, studied pre-law, met and married a mathematics student."

"Mary Smith," Johnny said, "known as Mollie." He nodded. "She's here now, and going to work at the Lab."

"That so?" The congressman did not seem much interested. "Anyway, Walter finished law school, never practiced, went with the FBI, got shunted around here and there, L.A., Dallas, Miami, finally here down in the city. Seems his jumping around didn't set well with his wife, and they were separated a year or so ago. Not divorced." The congressman had a swig from his shot glass. "End of story. Tell you anything?"

"It maybe explains the scar where the tattoo had been," Johnny said.

Hawley's eyebrows rose. "Hadn't thought of that," he said, and nodded. "Could be. Maybe joined a gang when he was a young kid, that kind of thing, you're thinking?"

"Possible." Johnny was silent, thinking about it. "Miami area, you said?" Bascomb also came from Miami. Coincidence? "I can ask the Miami police about the gangs they have."

"Far as his record with the Bureau," Mark Hawley said, "it's solid."

49

Johnny thought about that, too, and shook his head in mild disagreement. "Wallace, special agent in charge, Higgins's boss, said Higgins was sometimes a pain in the ass, a loose gun in a heavy sea."

Again the congressman's eyebrows rose. "That so? It's not on his record." He studied Johnny carefully. "You're thinking what?"

"Maybe," Johnny said slowly, "maybe it was only out here that he got wild ideas? How about that?"

The office was silent. Hawley picked up his glass, held it to the light, and admired the color of the liquor it contained. He set it down again. "You're thinking Bascomb? His being here set Higgins off?"

"Could be." Johnny paused. "Or maybe I'm just seeing Bascomb wherever I look. We don't know a thing against him." He emphasized the verb. He stood up then. "Thanks much," he said.

"De nada, son." The congressman was again studying his glass. He sighed. "Maybe I'd better ask a few questions myself about Bascomb." When he smiled, he resembled a crocodile in the shallows. "One of the benefits of being around Washington long as I have," he said, "is you pick up brownie points here and there. There's a couple of fellows from down Miami way owe me a few. I'll ask them to nose around some. Never can tell what might turn up, can you?"

Johnny nodded understandingly. "Sometimes," he said, "the woods are full of game that just takes flushing out."

Leon Bascomb paid a call on Will Carston—by careful, previous arrangement. On the telephone, Carston had been most cordial. "I shall be delighted to see you, Mr. Bascomb," he had said in his eastern-accented, cultured voice. "What time would be convenient for you?"

Will Carston had lived in Santo Cristo for over forty years. He was a poet (Pulitzer Prize) and the author of the monumental work on Spanish land grants published by the local university press. He lived very well on apparently inexhaustible inherited wealth, and was, among other things, a member of the museum board on which Leon Bascomb now also sat.

Carston's home, an old, sprawling, meticulously restored and maintained adobe house, was surrounded by eight acres of expensive Santo Cristo real estate, consisting of lawns, flower beds, cactus displays, and a fine kitchen vegetable garden, all enclosed by a seven-foot adobe wall in the top of which long-ago masons had thoughtfully placed broken glass to discourage intruders. The establishment required the full-time services of three gardeners, as well as inside help.

A maid met Bascomb at the heavy, carved front door and led him through the big house with its tiled and polished floors, its heavy, handcrafted furniture, and its expanses of whitewashed wall space on which paintings, mostly by southwestern artists and all of high quality, competed with an occasional museum-mounted southwestern Indian rug. Large windows cut into the massive walls gave glimpses of patios where fountains splashed, and tended borders of indigenous plants invited one to sink into the comfortable outdoor furniture and relax, totally removed from any sounds of traffic or neighborhood bustle.

Despite himself, Bascomb was impressed—and depressed as well by the sniggly feeling that against this quiet, cultured opulence, his own house and grounds would appear to have been put together yesterday morning, in haste. He disliked the feeling of inferiority he could not escape.

Carston was in his floor-to-beamed-ceiling-book-lined study, wearing even here in Santo Cristo's atmosphere of informality a long-sleeved shirt complete with gold cuff links, and a bow tie. He stood up to shake Bascomb's hand. "Sit down, please," he said. "Will you have tea, or would you prefer something a bit stronger?"

"Tea will be fine," Bascomb said. He detested tea.

"Now," Carston said as he waved the maid away and took his own chair, "to what do I owe the pleasure of this visit?" A faintly perceptible pause. "Museum business?"

"In a way." Bascomb, with effort, put the surroundings from his mind. "I have been wondering, do we—import from Mexico for the museum collection?"

Carston considered the question, and shook his head slowly. "Not really. On occasion, rare occasion, we have acquired—always with the full permission of the Mexican government—items that properly belong here in Santo Cristo, items that, for example, may have gone from here to Mexico for whatever reason, perhaps during the Pueblo Indian revolt of 1680 when the Spanish fled to El Paso and south." He paused. "Does that answer your question?"

Bascomb thought about it. "There is no—reciprocal arrangement?"

Carston smiled in his polite way. "Nothing formal. On occasion we have discovered that we had in our possession items that rightfully belonged below the border, items that perhaps had come into our hands by other than strictly ethical means, and those we have returned, meticulously, I hope and trust." Again Carston paused. "May I ask what prompts the questions?"

The old boy was sharp, Bascomb was thinking, but he was prepared for the query. "It is just that there is the similarity of cultures," he said smoothly, "and it seemed that there might well be some kind of exchange."

The maid arrived with a tray, a plate of sweets, silver tea service, and cups of such delicacy that Bascomb could see light clearly through their sides. Carston poured, and when he was finished and settled back in his chair again, teacup in hand, "Again on occasion," he said, "we have arranged loan exhibits both from and to Mexico. I have been involved in a number of them." He smiled wryly. "I am afraid such arrangements are not easily accomplished. There is . . . red tape involved. On both sides, I might add."

"Do you speak Spanish?" Bascomb said.

Carston smiled again. "Why, yes, Mr. Bascomb, I do. I decided that a rather thorough knowledge of the language was obligatory once I had decided to research the Spanish land grants here. I take it you have the language, too?"

"I was raised with both languages," Bascomb said. "My father was from Cuba."

"In long-ago times," Carston said, "I visited Cuba on a number of occasions." His smile this time was deprecatory. "Cuba and Bermuda were then as *de rigueur* for college students as Florida beach towns are now."

"I've never been there," Bascomb said. "Cuba, I mean. Or Bermuda, either, as far as that goes. My father had a shipping line sailing out of Miami, but I never was aboard one of his ships."

"Now, of course," Carston said, "one flies everywhere. Pity, in a way. The great ships plying between New York and Europe were very pleasant to travel on." He had a sip of his tea. "The inevitable question," he said, "because all of us are immigrants here in this culture. What brought you here, Mr. Bascomb?"

This, too, he had long been prepared for. "Miami climate, and too many people."

"Common complaints," Carston said. "We have Californians here because of the plethora of people in their own state, and also, of course, because earthquakes have become a cause for paranoia. We have Texans for a variety of reasons, and, of course, we have refugees from eastern winters, such as me." His voice altered subtly. "But we do not have many who have emigrated from Florida. Odd, don't you think?" He was smiling, but his eyes were appraising.

"I couldn't say. I can only speak for myself." Bascomb, too, sipped his tea, and refrained from making a face at the taste. "Back to the museum, or at least to a facet of it. I notice Mexican painters featured in some of our local galleries, and Mexican sculpture."

"And," Carston said, "you are wondering why the lack of commerce in older things?" He nodded. "The difference is vast, Mr. Bascomb. Mexico considers its ancient artifacts and artwork national treasures—as, indeed, they are. Modern artwork, however good or not so good, is still a—marketable commodity, and so the traffic exists." He dismissed the subject with a slight gesture. "More tea? No?" And then with no change of tone, "I have a faint knowledge of the Miami area. Tell me, where did you live there, Mr. Bascomb? And has the city changed much in, say, the last ten or fifteen years?"

When the same maid led Bascomb through the rooms and halls to the formal entrance where the gray Cadillac was parked, Bascomb was thinking that the old boy with his out-of-date manners had managed to ask at least as many questions as he answered, and Bascomb wondered why. Here in Santo Cristo, he was beginning to believe, there were a number of characters who were not exactly what he had anticipated finding in such a backwater. Food for thought.

Joe Todd, president of Todd Van & Storage, studied the list of carriers Bascomb had given him. There were van companies in Galveston, Houston, and New Orleans, as well as in cities farther north such as Chicago, Cleveland, and Syracuse. Obviously Bascomb's contacts within the moving company business were widespread; that went without saying.

More to the point was that Bascomb appeared to be on almost intimate terms with the management of each company on the list, because there were letters in the file inevitably beginning, "Dear Leon:" and going on to speak of past business arrangements, no doubt having to do with Bascomb's van & storage associations in Miami.

On the face of it, Todd could see no earthly reason against availing himself of the suggested part-load arrangements and distribution of the shipped goods, largely household effects, throughout southwestern New Mexico and Arizona, areas he knew intimately.

Why, then, was he even hesitating? Bascomb himself was the answer, he decided, and that was a very poor answer indeed.

Granted, Bascomb was not the kind of man with whom Todd was familiar. He was not a westerner, as his dress, speech, and manner amply proved. So? Santo Cristo was almost bulging with refugees from other parts of the country, and one took them for what they were, ignoring their previous backgrounds; this was the tradition of the West. What was that jingle that came out of Gold Rush times out in California?

> Oh, what was your name in the States?
> Was it Jackson or Johnson or Bates?
> Did you murder your wife
> And run for your life?
> Oh, what was your name in the States?

What one had been in the States did not matter then, nor did previous background really matter now. Lighten up, Joe, he told himself; just because you have some personal reservations about the man, if he can, as he has, show you the way to profitable business, why back off? Answer me that. There was no answer.

The matter settled, Joe Todd dictated a letter to be sent to each of the van companies on the list, thanking them for their offers of cooperation, and promising prompt and efficient handling of all consignments that might come his way. He had not realized before how simple the matter really was.

Charlie Cottrell, Cadillac dealer, turned up unexpectedly in Johnny's office. "I'm not here to try to sell you a Cadillac," he said, trying to keep it light, "or even an Oldsmobile." He was quite familiar with Johnny's four-wheel-drive pickup, as well as his modest tastes.

"Entendido, understood," Johnny said, and produced one of his rare smiles. "So what, then?"

Charlie slumped in his chair, his face a picture of consternation. "I'm damned if I know," he said. "Really *know,* I mean. All I've got is a far-out hunch that I don't much like."

Tony Lopez appeared and leaned against the wall to listen. The man, he decided, had come to the right place if he was dealing in hunches. The Indian was precisely the right *hombre* to communicate with on that wavelength.

Johnny said with no hint of impatience, "And what is your far-out hunch?"

"I heard a car door close." Charlie looked faintly embarrassed. "That's the hell of a silly thing, now, isn't it? When I say it aloud, I mean?"

Johnny's face could have been carved of stone, for all the expression it showed. "I don't know," he said. "Tell me the rest."

Charlie nodded as if accepting a command. "I've been around cars all my life," he said. "Worked back in Michigan at the GM factory, ran my own shop here before I managed to get into the dealership business. I know how to take cars apart and put them back together again—"

"So," Johnny said, "when you hear a car door close, you know how it ought to latch? Or sound?"

"Boy, howdy!" Charlie said admiringly. "You catch on quick, don't you?" He was silent for a few moments. "Used to be," he said, "you could almost judge a car's quality by the sound of its doors closing, you know what I mean? If they closed solid-like, with a good, tight sound, you pretty well knew that was how the rest of the car was built. If it closed with a light, rattling kind of sound, the way the old Model T's did, you knew you sure as hell weren't looking at a Duesenberg."

Still expressionless, "And this door?" Johnny said.

"Solid," Charlie said, "like a door closing on a safe, a big safe, like, maybe, the vault door closing in a bank—do you see what I mean?"

Johnny said slowly, "I think maybe I do. So what could cause a sound like that?"

"Only one thing." Charlie hesitated, obviously uncomfortable. He said at last, "Armor plate. I worked once on one of the White House cars. Same sound. When those doors closed—" Charlie shook his head. "—you knew that whoever was inside was all safe and snug in a thick, steel cocoon."

Johnny was silent for a few moments. "How would you make sure the car *was* armor-plated?" he said.

Charlie made a vague gesture. "Easiest would be to weigh it. Armor plate is heavy. Car like that weighs maybe twice what an ordinary model would, maybe three times."

Johnny said, "Do I have to ask whose car this was?"

"That," Charlie said, "is what worries me. Bascomb, he's my—partner." He paused. "Only people I know who go in for armored cars, aside from Brinks and Wells Fargo, are presidents of the United States, and Mafia bosses who want to keep healthy." He spread his hands helplessly.

"I see your problem," Johnny said, "but I don't

know what we can do. There's no law against a man owning whatever kind of car he wants."

"But at least now you know," Charlie said.

Johnny nodded again. All at once there was a harshness in his face that had not been there before. "Now we know," he agreed.

6

Lucille Harrington, martini in hand, sat on their *portal* admiring the evening view, which extended something over 100 miles to the massive shape of Mount Taylor clearly visible on the horizon.

Waldo Harrington sat nearby, he, too, with drink at hand. Music—a Schubert trio—played quietly on the record player inside the house.

Lucille said without preamble, "What do you think of Mollie Smith Higgins?" She spoke as almost always, in a quiet, uninflected voice that somehow projected her own quiet, calm, confident, and obviously competent personality. She was a large woman, strikingly handsome, with, when she chose to show it, a smile that could light up an entire room. Congressional committees had come to know that smile well as from time to time they listened and tried to follow Lucille's explanations of arcane and complicated matters of physics and mathematics.

"An enigma," Waldo said promptly. He spoke as if his tongue had difficulty keeping up with his mind. "No questioning her qualifications. Or her record in research." He sipped his drink thoughtfully.

Lucille looked at him with just the hint of a fond smile. "But?" she said.

"Now you see her," Waldo said with a small gesture, "and now you don't. In Washington they talk about budgetary smoke and mirrors. Mollie Smith could give them basic lessons in camouflage." He paused. "Or maybe protective coloration." He glanced at Lucille. "You asked the question with a purpose, no?"

Lucille studied distant Mount Taylor and spoke as if to it. "Her estranged husband is found murdered," she said, as if following a logical progression. "When Mollie is notified, she comes running. That, in itself, would not seem unusual. But she announces immediately that she has decided to stay here in Santo Cristo, where her husband was last seen alive." She turned from Mount Taylor then and looked at Waldo. "Does that suggest—anything?"

"Such as?"

Lucille took her time. She said at last, "There is an unexpected hard core to Mollie. Johnny told me a tale . . ." She recounted the story of the nighttime break-in and the results: the intruder's remains taken off in a body bag. She looked again at Mount Taylor. "An avenging Fury?" she said. "I daresay such things do happen, fiction aside."

Waldo was silent, contemplative.

"There is one thing more," Lucille said. "Johnny also told me that she was most anxious to claim her dead husband's wristwatch. It was a gift from her, she said."

Waldo's face showed mild surprise. "You find that unusual? Her wanting it as a keepsake, I mean?"

"Johnny did," Lucille said. "He had that enormous

bear of a man, Saul Pentland, go over it carefully. He found only a date on the back."

"Gifts frequently have dates, Lu." And, watching Lucille's face, he added, "What are you thinking?"

Lucille shook her head almost apologetically. "Just that—dates are numbers, a sequence of numbers, grouped."

"Oh, Lord!" Waldo said. "If you're thinking that way, Lu, you could be going in all kinds of directions —the combination of a safe, a numbered bank account, a telephone number, even an address . . ." He shook his head.

"Or a computer code," Lucille said. "And there may be others I haven't thought of yet."

Waldo finished his drink and sighed. "Have you told Johnny?"

"Not yet. I wanted to think about it."

Inside, the music faded slowly into silence. Waldo said, "The other side is another trio. Would you like to hear it?"

Lucille nodded. "With another martini." She paused, smiling. "While we think about numbers."

Mollie Smith had found a place to live. "It isn't much," she told Cassie in her shy, deprecatory way, "but it does have charm." Her voice altered subtly, turning practical. "And, I think, ample heat for winter." Immediately the practical tone disappeared. "And a fireplace, too."

"I'd love to see it."

"You will be my first guest."

At Mollie's house they sat in worn, comfortable, upholstered chairs in front of the piñon fire, the logs set on end in the local fashion. How many times had she and Johnny sat like this, staring at a fire? Cassie wondered, and then was curious to know why the question had even come to mind. Was there some similarity, however farfetched?

"You never knew my husband, did you?" Mollie said.

Cassie shook her head in silence. Was she about to hear reminiscences? They could be painful.

"He was a—driven man," Mollie said. She had put the shyness aside now. "What was driving him, I do not know." She looked then at Cassie. "I am good with numbers," she said, "concrete reasoning, A plus B equals C, that kind of thing." She paused. "I find people far more complex, totally unpredictable sometimes."

Cassie nodded, silent still.

"The last time I saw Walter," Mollie said, "he was . . . excited, as if he had just discovered something he had been looking for." She shook her head. "Again, I don't know what." The shy smile returned. "That was when I gave him his wristwatch." She paused. "I didn't know when I'd see him, so it wasn't even wrapped as a gift." This time there was an appreciable silence before she spoke again. "I'm afraid I wasn't much of a . . . wife," she said. "I know numbers, things, not people."

Cassie said slowly, "Do you want to tell me about him, Mollie?"

"What is there to tell? We met in college and were married while he was in law school and I was taking my graduate degree. I thought—" Mollie stopped.

Cassie waited, as she had seen Johnny do, because sooner or later a half-thought was likely to be completed. It was.

"I thought," Mollie said again, "that he would go into law practice and I would go into research, as I did, at the university." She looked at Cassie, and her eyes seemed to beg for understanding.

"Then," Cassie said, "you could have settled down to a real marriage? Was that it?"

Mollie nodded in silence. "Instead," she said, "he went with the Bureau. I told you he was *driven.*"

Again Cassie found herself thinking of Johnny as she stared at the piñon fire. "Driven" meant—what? Could the word be applied to Johnny when he was on a trail, all senses alert, all distractions ignored? Was that what Mollie had meant? And where did that thought come from?

Mollie said unexpectedly, "I suppose most couples talk about themselves to each other." The shy smile appeared. "Maybe I am wrong, but that is what I have always thought." The smile disappeared. She shook her head. "We never did. He was—he, and I was I, and it was almost as if we each began life in college. Unbelievable, or almost, when I think of it, but that is how it was."

"You never met his family?" Cassie's voice was gentle, understanding; she had never met any of Johnny's family, nor he hers.

Mollie's smile seemed turned inward, mocking herself. "He had a father," she said. "I never met him. He died." She paused, and the smile disappeared. "I had a mother," she said, and added instantly, "that is redundant, isn't it, everybody has a mother." Another pause. "She died." End of story.

Cassie heard herself saying automatically, inanely, "I'm sorry."

"Thank you. You are very kind." Mollie's voice was

again filled with shyness, as if she were afraid her words would be taken the wrong way.

"She is," Cassie told Johnny later that evening, again in front of a piñon fire, "a chameleon, the way she changes colors, moods. But I like her." Her smile mocked herself. "Maybe because we have a lot in common. We each came from—nowhere."

"Chica—"

"I know, Johnny," Cassie said softly. "It doesn't matter now, does it?"

Johnny talked on the phone with a Captain Vasquez of the Miami police. "Gangs we have," the captain said. "Maybe, what I hear, we're not quite in L.A.'s league, but gangs we got."

"Do they go in for tattoos?"

"And sometimes funny haircuts or red T-shirts or maybe bracelets or some damn thing."

"Does the tattoo of a snake ring a bell?"

The captain's voice altered. "Where?"

"On the right wrist."

There was a pause. "That," the captain said then, "goes back a ways, fifteen, maybe twenty years. Called themselves the Cobras. *Muy malo,* very bad. Finally got wiped out. Fact. Turf battle, and when it was over there weren't many Cobras left, which was a good thing."

"Thanks, Captain," Johnny said. "You've helped a lot."

"Anytime. I hear good things about your part of the world."

"We have our problems," Johnny said, "same as everybody else, I'm afraid."

"Ain't it the truth? *Es la vida,* that's life."

* * *

Jorge Trujillo again stood in Leon Bascomb's study to make his report. "The FBI guy," he said. "You wanted to know who he'd seen up here before he got himself dead."

"I did," Bascomb said. "I do."

"There's a cop," Jorge said. "Name of Ortiz." He saw the change in Bascomb's face. "You know him?"

"I've met him, yes. Go on. Higgins saw him?"

"The same day. They talked for a while. Not long. Then the FBI guy left."

Bascomb said slowly, carefully, "You are sure of this?"

"*Sí.*" Jorge smiled. "Cops like to drink, same as anybody else. The one I talked to had a loose mouth."

"You didn't talk to Ortiz, did you?"

Jorge shook his head. "No way. Around here they think he's a kind of *brujo,* a witch, part Indian, Apache. Nobody likes to mess with him."

Bascomb took a deep breath and let it out slowly. "Okay," he said. "That's it. Good job." And when Jorge had gone, carefully closing the study door after him, Bascomb swore softly in Spanish and then tried to put his thoughts in order.

He knew FBI routine, and it was rare indeed when agents bothered to check in with the local cops. He wondered why Higgins had. More important, he wondered how much Higgins might have told this Johnny Ortiz. Not enough, he decided, or he, Bascomb, would have had more than a call from Ortiz accompanied by that old rancher Ben Hart, and there would have been pointed questions instead of mere innuendo. By that much, Bascomb felt better.

On the other hand, there was really no way of telling how much Ortiz might know, was there? And that left a loose end hanging. Bascomb disliked loose ends, and usually had ways of dealing with them. But a local cop? It wanted, no, it *demanded* thinking about.

Will Carston paid a call on Cassie at the museum. "Just passing by, my dear," he said, "and thought I would drop in." Not true, but it would serve, Carston thought. There were definite advantages to age.

"I am flattered," Cassie said, and meant it. The old gentleman was a potent force in the museum hierarchy. There had been changes over the few years Cassie had been associated with the institution, but Will Carston's position, like that of a sturdy pillar supporting the roof, had never even been in question.

"Mr. Leon Bascomb paid me a call," Carston said as he settled himself comfortably on the straight visitor's chair. Chico emerged from beneath Cassie's desk and graciously accepted Carston's gentle scratching beneath his chin. His tail thumped the floor in gratitude. "An interesting man," Carston added in a manner that was perhaps too casual. His face was bland and expressionless.

Cassie said carefully, "He seems to have attracted considerable attention in Santo Cristo."

Carston's fingers continued their gentle scratching of Chico's chin. "There are some who move here," he said, "who seem to fit in at once. Others never quite seem at ease." He smiled gently. "Some of those, of course, are stunned by the vast expanses of this country, the openness, the mountains that look down. They feel, I have come to believe, as if God is watching them constantly, and there is no place to hide."

Cassie's laugh was light and easy. "You may have the answer," she said. "If and when they can, they choose an arroyo with no view in any direction."

"And they have tiny windows installed," Carston said. "Yes." He was silent for a moment. "Others build glass houses, and then give the impression that they are afraid of stones being thrown." He paused again. "What is your assessment, my dear, of Mr. Bascomb?"

Cassie shook her head slowly, unsmiling now. "I am not sure."

"Precisely." Carston's voice was uninflected. He took his time before he went on. "He appeared to believe," he said at last, "that there might be benefit in a . . . I suppose *traffic* is the word, between us and Mexico." He looked at Cassie then and waited in his quiet, courteous way.

Cassie said carefully, "What kind of traffic?"

"He was not specific," Carston said, "but I rather gathered that he was thinking in terms of old artwork and perhaps artifacts as well." He paused. "A one-way traffic, of course."

"We have had that before," Cassie said, and an edge had crept into her tone.

Carston nodded. "Perhaps that is why it came so readily to mind when I listened to him."

Cassie shook her head in unhappy silence.

"There *is* a market for such items, my dear," Carston said. "You must be aware of that. There are unscrupulous collectors willing to pay large sums for such items as pre-Columbian jewelry, statuary, carvings, and such. Have you any idea what the collection from Tomb 7 at Monte Alban might bring on the illegal market? I should put the figure in the millions."

"That is beyond my understanding," Cassie said, and meant it.

"Because you are an ethical and honest person." Carston nodded. "And yet a Van Gogh disappears, a work comparable to paintings of his that have already brought millions at auction—and is never seen again, except by the unscrupulous collector who hoards it as a miser hoards his gold."

Cassie took a deep breath and let it out slowly. "I have to believe you are right," she said. "But here—he—is that actually what you think he might have in mind?"

"Merely a whiff of suspicion, my dear, but one that I intend to keep in mind. And just between us."

Cassie hesitated. "Johnny . . ." she began.

"If you would care to pass my whiff of suspicion along to him," Carston said, "please feel free to do so. I would value his opinion." He gave Chico a final pat on the head and stood up. "Thank you for your attention, my dear," he said. "It is always a pleasure to see you and talk with you. *Hasta luego,* until we meet again."

"Hasta luego," Cassie said, and added, also in Spanish, "Go with God."

She recounted her conversation with Will Carston to Johnny that evening. His reaction was not quite what she'd expected.

He stared at the fire for some time in silence, and said at last, "Could be, I suppose." Turning to look directly at Cassie, he added, "But somehow I doubt it. It—doesn't have quite the right feel."

Cassie said gently, "Can you explain that?"

Johnny took his time. He said at last, "Will Carston is right, of course. He usually is. There *is* traffic in illegal art, *and* artifacts, treasures, that kind of thing. And there's money to be made, no doubt about it." He paused. "But it's not the . . . violent kind of crime, as far as I know. It doesn't go with submachine guns or a killing rage." He smiled without amusement. "And I don't see its needing an armor-plated car to run around in, either."

Cassie thought about it. "When you think of those things," she said, "guns, armored cars, what does come to mind?"

"These days," Johnny said slowly, "only one thing —drugs. Willie Sutton said the reason he robbed banks was because that was where the money was. Today the money's in cocaine, heroin, crack, amphetamines. Banks are almost out of style." His face turned harsh. "And drugs is where the violence is, too. Not the sudden, impulsive violence, the Saturday-night argument that ends with somebody being knifed or shot, but the systematic, you-get-in-my-way-and-I-waste-you, run-of-the-mill, every day and every night, routine kind of violence."

Cassie said slowly, incredulously, "Leon Bascomb?"

"I don't know, *chica*. And that is a fact. So far I can't see any connection. I'm walking blind in unfamiliar woods."

Once, Cassie was remembering, she had heard someone say that Johnny would track a spirit through hell and pick up its tangible tracks again on the other side. Watching his face now, she could believe it. She said, "Sometimes you almost frighten me. You really do. Did you know that?"

Johnny's face softened, and his voice turned gentle. "I don't mean to, *chica*. Not ever. Believe that."

7

Leon Bascomb had a phone call from Miami. The voice, speaking English, was crisp and authoritative. "A couple people asking questions about you," the voice said. "You know why?"

"No idea," Bascomb said, "but *no importa.*"

"Maybe yes, maybe no, but I don't like it."

Neither did Bascomb, but no doubt sounded in his voice. "Who?" he said. "And what questions?"

"Local heat. But it's who's behind them that counts. Two congressmen. Local heat we can handle. Washington is something else. What I want to know is why."

Bascomb stared at the far wall. "I'll see what I can find out."

"You do that." The voice paused. "This whole deal was your idea, remember?"

"I remember."

"And if it goes sour, it's your ass. Remember that, too." Again the voice paused. "You want help? Maybe a little muscle?"

"No."

"Maybe Artie," the voice said. "He's handy to have around, case you need a little chore done."

"This is a small town," Bascomb said, thinking that Artie might stand out like a sore thumb.

"So you told me. Then why is Washington interested? Tell me that."

Bascomb could not help smiling at the implied sense of insularity. "We have congressmen, too," he said. "Even way out here." And the moment the words were out, he began to see the connection, and did not like it even a little bit. "Artie," he said suddenly. "Yes. Maybe Artie would be a good idea at that."

"You got ideas?" There was new interest in the voice.

"I'm beginning to get them," Bascomb said. "I'll be in touch."

"Artie'll be on his way this afternoon." The line went dead.

Bascomb hung up and sat quiet, staring at the far wall. Of course, of course. Old Mark Hawley, congressman. And in a town this size, everybody knew everybody else, or near enough. Old Ben Hart and Hawley were great buddies, no? Yes. And the Ortiz cop knew Ben Hart well; that had been made plain enough. So most likely he also knew the congressman. And that could, and probably did, explain the Washington interest.

Every time he turned around, Bascomb was beginning to think, there was Ortiz looking at him, and that made the cop no longer just a loose end; it made him a nuisance—one that Artie could take care of. They didn't come any better than Artie at dealing with nuisances who caused problems.

* * *

INTERLOPER

Joe Todd stared again at the monthly balance sheet and found it hard to believe. There were no figures in parentheses indicating losses, none. There were only lovely, healthy figures indicating profit, full loads for his moving vans, full-time occupation for his drivers, and lucrative storage arrangements for some part-loads of household goods while they waited for space for transshipment.

Leon Bascomb had been right; folks were moving west in hordes, from New York, Florida, Louisiana, Mississippi, Texas, and even from Illinois, as if they simply could not wait to get into California's fabled sunshine—not to mention Los Angeles's smog and crowded freeways. No matter; if folks wanted to move, that was their business, and Joe Todd's.

At this rate, he was thinking, he was going to need at least one new van, or at least a semi-trailer without tractor to be loaded and made ready to roll just as soon as a westbound long-haul van came in, its load to be broken up into easily deliverable portions for destinations scattered through northern New Mexico and southern Colorado. Maybe, he thought, even two new semi-trailers, and at least one new man on the payroll to handle the transshipments.

He had talked on the phone with a couple of the moving van people who were sending him these part-loads, and all of them had agreed with the fellow in Houston with the Texas drawl, who had said, "A full load we'll take anywhere and hope to pick up a load coming back. That makes money sense. But these part-loads for places out in the Arizona boonies or little towns nobody ever heard of in California are nothing but damned headaches. We haul them to you and let you spread them out, knowing the territory like you do, and everybody's happy, right?"

73

"In spades," Joe had said. "Good for you. Good for me."

The only thing was, why hadn't he thought of this sooner? So, okay, the answer to that was clear, too: He hadn't had the connections Leon Bascomb obviously had clear across the country to the East Coast. How lucky could Joe Todd get, having Bascomb like the good fairy in the storybooks appearing just when he was needed?

Lucille and Waldo Harrington came together to see Johnny. "Lu," Waldo said, "has been thinking." He said it almost apologetically, as if thinking were something shameful. "And," he added in his quick way, "maybe she has something at that."

"Just maybe," Lucille said, and turned on that smile that could, and did, light up the entire office. "Numbers," she said, "as on the back of a watch."

Johnny's eyebrows rose. "Higgins's watch?" he said.

"Exactly." Lucille paused. "At first, I'll admit the idea did seem farfetched, no more than a wild guess based on supposition. Then I talked to Cassie, and something Mollie Higgins had told her made me wonder even more. So I talked with Mollie myself."

"That," Waldo said, "was when it began to make some kind of sense."

Johnny said quietly, "Go on."

"Mollie," Lucille said, "told Cassie that she hadn't known when she would see Higgins, so she didn't even have the watch wrapped." She paused. "She hadn't had it engraved, either."

Johnny's face was masklike. He sat silent, waiting.

"So Higgins had the engraving done himself," Lucille Harrington said. "And the date, if it is a date, is not the date on which Mollie gave him the watch, nor is it his birthday or any other significant date that Mollie recognizes. We thought you ought to know."

Johnny produced one of his rare smiles. "Any ideas?" he said.

Lucille shook her head. "At the moment, none." Again she paused. "But numbers are in a sense our business. And Mollie's, and maybe, just maybe, among the three of us we will be able to make some sense out of them. Obviously they are on the watch for a reason, don't you think?"

"I think," Johnny said, "that we can take that as fact." And he added, "My thanks."

He sat for a long time, unmoving, after Lucille and Waldo had left. The picture he had formed of Higgins was of a secretive man, presumably possessed of considerable intelligence. If the numbers on the back of the watch had significance, and Johnny had no doubt that they had, then either they were there as a reminder for Higgins himself or, and this seemed the more logical possibility, as a message of some kind. To whom? Most likely Mollie, no?—his next of kin, to whom his watch would eventually be given if he, Higgins, met with an accident.

So far, so good, but beyond that Johnny could not go, and he would leave the matter where it was, in more capable hands than his own, for possible solution. *Bueno.*

That night, sitting in front of the fire with Cassie, Chico at their feet, Johnny told about the visit by the Harringtons. "Very bright people," he said. "If anyone can figure out what the numbers mean, if anything, and I can't think otherwise, then they will."

Cassie said, "Do you know the numbers?"

"12-22-88," Johnny said without hesitation. "Normally that would mean December 22, 1988, no? But that wasn't the date Mollie gave Higgins the watch, and it wasn't his birthday or their wedding anniversary or anything else that seems to mean something. So what are they?"

"They sound like the combination to a safe."

"Possible." Johnny stood up. "Let's leave it like that, *chica*. People are my thing, not numbers."

Cassie smiled. "Mollie Higgins said precisely the opposite about herself. Funny, isn't it?"

There were three gallery openings that following Saturday, and Leon Bascomb, in his role of art patron, attended them all. It was at the third, at The Gallery, that he met Mollie Higgins, or, more accurately, that Mollie Higgins introduced herself to him.

"I have heard a great deal about you," Mollie said in her shy, diffident way, almost as if apologizing for intruding on his apparent study of the exhibited pieces of Una Hanbury sculpture.

Bascomb smiled in an automatic way. "Nothing bad, I hope?" He was to remember later that she did not answer the question.

Instead, "My name is Mollie Higgins," she said. "Walter Higgins was my husband." The shy tone remained, but Mollie's eyes held a strange intensity as she watched Bascomb's face.

Bascomb appeared to think. "I don't believe I know the name," he said. "Sorry."

Mollie indicated the superb bronze sculpture of three mountain goats gathered on a narrow, rocky ledge, completely at ease perhaps a thousand feet above a yawning gorge. "Lovely, aren't they?" she said. "They seem so friendly." And then, with no change of tone, "In many ways Walter was a strange

76

man, Mr. Bascomb, even at times a bit difficult to get along with."

"Is that so?" Bascomb's voice indicated complete lack of interest.

"He kept his thoughts very much to himself," Mollie said, "but the last time I saw him I—sensed that he was quite excited." Her smile was apologetic. "I could only believe that he had discovered something he had been searching for for a long time."

"Interesting, I'm sure," Bascomb said, and moved on to the next piece of sculpture, of three small bronze owls looking so real you were tempted to stroke their feathers.

Mollie moved with him. "When Walter was found," she said, "his body had been—stripped of all personal possessions except one, his wristwatch that I had given him."

Bascomb stared fixedly at the owls and said nothing.

"Strange," Mollie said in a musing tone that now lacked diffidence, "because there were numbers engraved on the back of the watch. Walter had had them engraved there. Why, I don't know, because although they seem to be a date, month, day, and year, they do not refer to any date I recognize." Again the apologetic smile, and the shy tone had returned. "I mean, as his wife, you would think I would know what the date refers to, wouldn't you, Mr. Bascomb?"

"I'm not married," Bascomb said, "so I really couldn't say. And now, if you will excuse me—"

"Of course," Mollie said quickly. "I do hope I haven't intruded on your enjoyment of the exhibit. I wouldn't like to think I have been a nuisance." She scurried off and was lost in the crowd where Cassie waited.

Bascomb looked thoughtfully at her disappearing back. His face was expressionless.

"I spoke to him," Mollie told Cassie in a slightly breathless voice.

"I think we might go now," Cassie said. "An opening is really not the time to see the artwork. Besides, I don't think it's good to let him see us together."

Congressman Mark Hawley said, "Word I get from down Miami way is that far as anybody knows, Bascomb is clean. His father came from Cuba and built himself a shoestring shipping company, freighters that carried mostly piggyback cargoes, the kind you load on flatcars or on flatbed trucks, you know what I mean?"

Johnny nodded. "Cargo from where?"

"You name it, Gulf ports, Mexico, South America, the Caribbean—" The congressman spread his hands. "Father went broke, belly-up maybe ten years ago. That's when Leon Bascomb first appears, young, good with figures, smart, industrious. Father died. Son took over what was left of the shipping company, salvaged maybe a few thousand dollars, then sort of dropped out of sight."

The congressman had a sip of whisky. "About six years ago he turns up again with more than just walking-around money to invest in real estate, a moving-van company with nationwide connections, a good-sized house, a nightclub—all open and above-board. No known mob connections, no scandals, Mister Clean."

"Women?" Johnny said.

Mark Hawley shook his head. "No women. No

what they call these days gay connections, either. The cat that walks by himself."

"Is it known where his money came from?"

"Other investments—he says, if asked. The Bahamas, Jamaica, some Texas oil leases that paid off, that kind of thing." The congressman shook his head. "Sorry, son. I'd hoped, like you did, that maybe something would turn up on his record, but not even the IRS has a hint of anything out of line." The congressman showed his teeth in his crocodile-in-the-shallows smile. "I called in a few markers with them, too."

"Thanks," Johnny said.

"You still like him, don't you, son?"

"Just a feeling. Higgins was interested in him. He drives an armor-plated car." Johnny shrugged. "Of course, there are all kinds of innocent explanations."

"But you don't believe them, is that it?"

Johnny smiled. "Like I said, just a feeling, like maybe you've seen some vague tracks, could be old, could have been made ten minutes ago—and somehow you are suddenly pretty damn sure that around the next corner there's a big bull elk just waiting for you to spot him." Smiling still, he shook his head. "But just as often as not, there isn't any elk. Not around the next corner, not around the corner after that. You imagined the whole thing." He stood up. "Thanks for the try."

"Anytime, son. With your batting average, I tend to go along with your hunches."

Artie—his last name was Gilmore, or at least that was the name on his driver's license and credit cards—out from Miami, driving a rented car, met with Bascomb some miles out of town on a lonely road just outside Ben Hart's ranch boundaries. Artie was a quiet man who smiled seldom, and whose eyes were rarely still, as if they perpetually searched for danger. "This local cop," he said, "tell me about him."

"Part Indian," Bascomb said, "part Hispanic, part Anglo. Middle-sized, sharp, and by all accounts dangerous."

The corner of Artie's mouth lifted slightly, indicating amused skepticism, but he said nothing.

"How much he knows," Bascomb said, "I have no idea." He was having second thoughts. "So maybe we might wait a bit to see what happens next."

"Why wait?" Artie said. "He's a nuisance? Okay. I take him out of the action before he makes trouble." There was finality in his tone. "What kind of car does he drive?"

"A four-wheel-drive pickup."

"Got it," Artie said. "See you." He got back into his rented car.

Bascomb rolled up the Cadillac's tinted window and sat quiet for a little time, watching Artie's trail of dust dissipate gradually, before he put the big car in gear and drove off slowly. He was unaware that Ben Hart, on horseback and almost invisible in a dip of his land, attracted by the dust plumes the two cars had raised, was watching through binoculars.

As he drove back into town, Bascomb was thinking of small Mollie Higgins and that curious confrontation at the art gallery. He had not known about the wristwatch—hadn't Jorge said he had removed everything?—and he was not sure he liked the idea of numbers engraved on its back. It would be well, he thought, if he knew what those numbers were. Jorge, having overlooked the watch in the first place, could damn well find out.

On the phone, "Big city dude, I'd say," Ben Hart said, and snorted. "Wore gold chains around his neck. Will you tell me what that's supposed to mean?"

Johnny could smile at the old man's obvious scorn. "They show what a big fellow you are," he said. "Like wearing a diamond pinky ring. What kind of car was he driving?"

"Blue. One of those new ones, a sedan, they all look alike." Ben himself drove a great, dusty Cadillac known to every state cop in the area. "May mean nothing at all," Ben said, "but they sure as hell picked a lonely spot to get together, and I wondered why." He paused. "Mean-looking *hombre,* gold chains or no, so was I you, I'd look back over my shoulder every now and again."

"Thanks, Ben. I will." Johnny hung up and thought for a moment or two before he went out to his pickup, took the 30-30 carbine from its rack across the rear window, and laid it on the floor partway beneath the seat.

He did not tell Cassie that night what Ben had seen. Nor did he tell her that a blue sedan had followed him when he drove home. The sedan did not stop when Johnny turned into their drive, but went on its way as if it knew its destination.

Tomorrow, Johnny thought, would be another day, but it would be just as well to be prepared for it, so after dinner that night he went pub-crawling.

Santo Cristo is not a night town. Except during opera, chamber music, and off-again-on-again repertory theater seasons, there is little to do after dark, and *turistas* tend to gravitate to Arroyo Road, which is devoted largely to bars, coffee shops, and restaurants sandwiched between galleries and arts and crafts shops. It was there that Johnny launched his reconnaissance.

He began at El Tecolote y El Gatito, run by a young woman named Sam, small, usually crowded, its walls decorated with murals depicting the owl and the pussycat in various situations. Sam, behind the bar, saw Johnny come in and shook her head in mock protest.

"Migod, the fuzz," she said. "What have we done now?"

"As far as I know, Sam," Johnny said, "nothing out of the ordinary." He liked Sam. She was what she was and made no bones about it, and if her sexual preferences were not Johnny's or Cassie's, why, what difference?

"Then," Sam said, "you're looking for somebody. I can see the glint in your eye. Who this time?"

"Any strangers?"

Sam waved one hand to indicate the entire crowded room. "About half are *turistas,* I'd say. Anyone in particular?"

Sam could, and did, keep her mouth shut. "Any wearing gold chains?" Johnny said. "Probably a big city dude?"

Sam's face altered expression. "That one," she said, and nodded. "He was here, had a drink, went on up the street. He a baddo?"

"I wouldn't know, Sam. But he interests me."

"Rather him than me," Sam said. "Good hunting."

Johnny drew a blank at El Portal, which was a coffee shop with chess tables and (by airmail daily) copies of the *New York Times* and *Variety.* Ditto Eddie's restaurant and the Torremolinas bar next door. It was at El

Rincôn that he saw Artie standing alone at the bar, watching the room behind him in the backbar mirror.

Johnny, unseen in the darkness outside, paused only a moment and then walked on, a picture of the man indelibly etched in memory—a mean-looking *hombre,* as Ben Hart had said, sure of himself even in these unfamiliar surroundings, wearing a jacket, as most in the bar were not, an open sports shirt showing a mat of black chest hair, the two or three gold chains Ben had noted, and pointed shoes with built-up heels brilliantly polished.

Basta, enough; Johnny had had his look and that was all that mattered. He went on home in his unhurried way to Chico, a warm bed, and Cassie.

8

Little Mollie Smith Higgins sat in the living room of her rented house and, one by one, examined the pitiful remnants of Walter Higgins's life as contained in the box Wallace, FBI special agent in charge, had been good enough to collect and send to her.

At her request, Walter's clothing had been donated to Goodwill, so at least, she thought, she did not have to face the trauma of dealing with that.

But here was a framed picture of her, taken the day of their wedding; and the pen-and-pencil desk set that had been her wedding gift to Walter; a metal box of papers she would go through at her leisure; a dictionary and the old portable typewriter on which Walter had pecked with two fingers; a *Black's Law Dictionary;* an attaché case he had rarely used; his electric shaver and the comb and brush she remembered so vividly because they, too, had been her gift; an envelope of keys, each meticulously tagged and marked with its purpose; the compact personal computer she had almost had to force him to buy and had taught him to use; the old watch her gift had replaced; a hunting knife, relic of some long-ago summer spent as a boy in the Michigan woods; his small, electric travel clock; a flashlight; a pair of binoculars; and a 35mm SLR camera showing on its frame counter that seventeen frames had been exposed, so presumably film was still in it . . .

She had the box emptied at last and, looking at the pile of things, began to cry, which was a silly thing to do, she told herself, but found that she could not stop.

Walter was the only man she had ever known intimately, or even well. During their separation she had missed him—witness the watch she had bought for him as an unexpected gift—but somehow the fact of death, so final a state, affected her far more than she would have expected, and she was not now quite certain how she would manage to cope. Once her security check was completed, she would have her work up at the Lab, of course, as she had had back at the university, and that would help to occupy her.

And there was Cassie Enright, whom she had come to like immensely, and those dear people the Harringtons, so, in effect, for the first time in her adult life, except for those few months with Walter, she did not find herself alone. Here in Santo Cristo she could, and would, find a new life.

Still the tears would not stop.

She decided a good hot bath might help, and then perhaps a cup of hot chocolate before bed, and she left the things from the box where she had put them, turned out the living room lights, and went into the rear of the little house.

She was in bed, sleeping peacefully, the tears at last subdued, when she was awakened by faint sounds coming from the living room.

She lay quiet for a few moments, gathering herself, and then, noiselessly, slipped out of bed, put on her robe, took from the bedside table the .25 Banker's Special automatic Walter had given her, and, in bare feet, crossed the small bedroom and opened the door.

There was a man with a flashlight bending over the pile of Walter's things, pawing through them with his free hand.

What Mollie felt, aside from fear she could and did control, was a sense of outrage that sounded clearly in her voice as she said loudly, "Who are you and what do you want?"

Instantly the flashlight was turned in her direction, temporarily blinding her, and almost simultaneously, as the man saw the gun in her hand, the light went dark. There were sounds of hurried footsteps, the outside door opened, and the man ran out into the night. Moments later, obviously at some little distance, a car's engine started up and wheels spun in the dirt as the car sped away.

Mollie was trembling as she crossed the room, closed and carefully locked the door, and then for a brief time leaned against it feeling a sense of weakness in her knees along with the sense of outrage that continued unabated.

"They were Walter's things," Mollie told Cassie the next morning, "and now they are mine, and I felt somehow . . . violated by his pawing through them."

Anger instead of fear, Cassie was thinking, and again found herself admiring little Mollie Higgins, who was very far indeed from the fearful desert pocket mouse Johnny had originally supposed her to be. "I think," Cassie said, "that we'd better go see Johnny. I doubt if this was just a simple burglary attempt."

Johnny agreed. "The door was locked?" he said.

"Definitely," Mollie said.

"Then we're not dealing with a kid with larceny in mind, but with a pro. And we don't have many professional housebreakers around here. Our problems are mostly snatch-and-run." He got up from his chair. "Let's have a look."

"Nothing was taken," Mollie said in mild protest.

Johnny produced what passed for a smile. "But something may have been left. We'll see."

Something had been left, as Johnny pointed out. "Those are boot-tracks. He was in no hurry coming to the door. He was in a big hurry when he left. Yes, here is where his car was parked, already headed away. This was no amateur."

Cassie said, "We think we know what he was after." She told Johnny of Mollie's conversation with Bascomb about the numbers on Higgins's watch at The Gallery art opening. "Doesn't it make sense that that was what they were after?"

"Could be," Johnny said. "Probably is. But we have no proof of a tie-in." He was silent for a moment, looking from Mollie to Cassie in a meaningful way. "Until we know something definite," he said at last, "I think you two had better not try any more attempts at flushing game out of the brush. A bear might come out, and bears are dangerous."

"I am angry," Mollie said. The shyness was entirely gone.

There was a hint of a smile on Cassie's lips as she watched Johnny for reaction.

"I don't blame you," Johnny said. "But I think you'd better let me handle it anyway."

Mollie shook her head. "I want to do something. He was my husband."

"Then," Johnny said, "try to figure out what, if anything, the numbers on the watch mean. That's your territory, isn't it? Numbers, I mean?"

"Very well." Mollie's voice was firm. "I haven't gone through Walter's papers yet. I will. And there is exposed film in his camera."

"Good girl," Johnny said, and meant it.

He drove Cassie back to the museum. "You're waiting for me to say it," he said after a silence, and his smile was sheepish. "All right. She is quite a pocket mouse." He shook his head. "More like a desert ferret. They will fight anything that threatens." His eye was on the rearview mirror. The blue sedan was following. *Bueno.* He held the door for Cassie. "Take care, *chica.* I don't want anything to happen to you." He felt better when he saw her disappear into the building. Now, he thought, we'll see about goldchains. As he drove away, he reached for the radio microphone.

To Tony Lopez, summoned to the radio at headquarters, "I'm being followed," Johnny said. "I'm going to take a little ride and see what he has in mind. He's the *hombre* Ben Hart mentioned."

"Do you want backup?"

Johnny smiled, and then his face settled into its harsh, Indian lines. "No. I think I can handle it. Over and out."

Tony handed the microphone to Callahan, the desk sergeant. "God help him," he said, "whoever he is."

In the blue sedan, Artie Gilmore drove competently, relaxed at the wheel. There was little traffic and he had no problem keeping Johnny's pickup in sight. Hicktown county-mountie types like this, he thought, acted as if they owned the world and all they had to do was snap their fingers to bring everybody into line.

This one didn't even carry a gun. There was a rack across the rear window of the pickup, the kind of rack in which Artie had seen masons carrying their levels, and maybe out here in the sticks they used them to carry long guns, too, but the pickup's rack was empty. Well, the hicktown cop was in for a surprise.

The pickup appeared to have a destination out in the boonies, because they left the city behind and took a minor, surfaced road that wound climbing through the rolling countryside dotted with piñon and juniper, with here and there a cholla cactus looking, Artie thought, like it was being tortured, the way its branches seemed to writhe in impossible curving lines.

Presently, as they climbed, the piñon and juniper disappeared, replaced by towering pine trees whose scent filled the air. Here and there among the trees Artie could see funny-looking greenish-colored tree trunks and leaves that shimmered in invisible wind currents. They were aspens, but Artie neither knew nor cared.

The road turned to dirt, but continued to climb steadily. Some of the curves were blind, but inevitably when he came around the bend, Artie could again see the pickup rolling along and raising a dust trail at a leisurely pace, as if the cop at the wheel was out for a trip in the country just admiring the scenery.

They topped a rise, in reality a pass, and started downgrade, and here all at once the scenery was different, without trees of any kind, only rocks carved into strange formations by wind and rain and changing temperatures until they resembled castles with turrets and parapets like Artie had seen in pictures.

A man had to have a hole in his head, Artie thought, to want to live in a land like this without buildings or people or other cars or anything at all except those big, damn rocks and space that reached to infinity beneath a cloudless sky in which the sun was like a spotlight, only hotter, despite the blue sedan's air-conditioning.

The dirt road stretched empty for miles, the pickup rolled along at its own pace, and Artie wondered if the hick cop even knew that there was another car behind him. Probably not; why bother to look in the mirror on a road like this?

It was a long time before they approached a curve in the road where a towering, sheer wall of red rock had defied road engineering. The pickup disappeared around the curve and Artie followed at his chosen distance, but suddenly, around the curve the scenario had changed.

The pickup was stopped off the road in an open stretch of dirt hard against the great, red rocks. And it was empty, the hick cop nowhere to be seen.

Artie slowed the sedan and brought it to a stop beside the pickup. When he opened the door and slid out into the sudden heat of the day, there was a gun in his hand, and his eyes searched restlessly and saw nothing but dirt, rock, the distant, infinite horizon, and the cloudless sky in which the sun burned like a focused torch, its heat all at once a burdensome weight on Artie's shoulders and bare head.

The damn cop had simply disappeared. This was Artie's first thought. Maybe, even probably he had finally noticed the car behind him and decided to— what? Make a run for it? What else? Why, hell, it could be as simple as the cop wanting to take a pee, couldn't it? But why disappear? There hadn't been any traffic; nobody to see—except Artie. And all this space, all this emptiness, nobody at all to watch what happened, couldn't have been better, could it? The weight of the gun in his hand was comforting. So, okay, hick cop, you want to play hide-and-seek? Fine. I'll play.

Looking restlessly from side to side, Artie crossed the stretch of dirt toward what looked to be an opening in the rock. It was: a passage, sand-and-dirt-covered, looking as if once it had been a path of some kind, as, indeed, it had, an ancient path, old before Columbus encountered the New World.

Sheer rock walls rose on either side, dotted here and there with small openings, wind-eroded. There was little brush and no trees, and the sun seemed to concentrate its heavy heat within the rock walls as in a furnace. Artie was sweating now, and the jacket he wore to hide the shoulder holster had become a burden difficult to bear. The gold chains themselves seemed to have absorbed the heat, too; they were suddenly uncomfortable around his neck.

Warily he walked on, searching every side turning, every cave opening, every clump of brush. And the farther he walked, the hotter the enclosing rock seemed to become. He had walked a hundred yards, two hundred, and seen nothing, and his built-up shoes, comfortable enough on city sidewalks, slipped in the loose sand and dirt, and somehow small, sharp pebbles had worked their way into the shoes and were punishing his feet through his thin socks.

He was beginning to wonder now if maybe the hick cop, the county-mountie, had had more in mind than he, Artie, had bargained for. So, okay, if it was games they were playing, the end was still never in doubt. Artie had played this kind of hunting game before and inevitably come out on top. His hand that held the gun was steady, and his eyes, despite the sweat that trickled into them, never ceased their restless searching. Come on, he thought; *damn you, come on!*

The sudden sound of the rifle shot was impossibly loud as it echoed and reverberated within the rock walls. Dirt and sand flew between Artie's feet, and the sound of the ricocheting bullet whined in his ears. Behind him there was the unmistakable sound of a shell being levered into place, and Johnny's voice said, "Drop the gun and turn around slowly, your hands behind your head. Or, don't. Your choice. But that was just a warning, and the next shot won't be. I'm through playing games."

Artie stood quite still, trying hard to think. He had no idea how the goddamn cop had managed to get behind him, but there was no doubt that he was there. And the memory of the painful impact of sand and dirt on his ankles and the sound of the ricocheting bullet were very vivid.

"Make up your mind," Johnny said. His voice was cold, relentless. "You're here in my country, *hombre*. And I wear the badge. And I'll gun you down without even thinking twice. So make up your mind. I'm losing patience."

Artie dropped the gun. He put his hands behind his head and turned slowly. Johnny was thirty feet away, the 30-30 carbine held waist-high pointing straight at Artie's belly. "Now move back a few feet," Johnny said, "and we'll have a little talk."

Artie moved back. He stopped. "Talk?" he said. "Screw you."

Johnny smiled. It was not a pleasant smile. "Oh, you'll talk," he said easily.

"Look," Artie said, "I know my rights. You can lock me up—"

Johnny shook his head. "I won't lock you up. I won't even take you in. I'll just leave you here." His tone was conversational. *"Turista* takes a drive in the country. His car breaks down. Nobody comes here. You might last the rest of the day. You might even last the night and part of tomorrow. Then the vultures and the skunks and the ravens will pick your bones clean. Eventually someone will find what's left. We lose somebody out here every now and again. You can believe that."

"Damn you, I have my rights—"

"Wrong," Johnny said. His voice now was cold. "You left your rights back when we left town. Out here you're just vulture meat. You think you can walk out? In those shoes? You, a big-city dude? You might get a mile. But there are thirty more beyond that, and the sun will kill you long before you even begin to make them."

Artie thought of all the empty country they had driven through. Walk that distance? No way. The goddamn cop had it right; Artie *might* make a mile, but in that sun, that heat, that emptiness—then what?

And the cop wasn't even sweating. How could that be? And what was in his eyes, which looked like chips of some shiny, black stone, was something he had never seen before, not even in Miami's hard world.

"You're wondering if I mean what I say," Johnny said. "I do. My ancestors staked *gringos* like you out on anthills, naked and smeared with honey, and watched the ants pick them clean. I won't bother to do that. I'll let the sun do it for me." He paused. "Unless we have that little talk I mentioned."

Jesus, Artie thought, the man means what he says, and an empty feeling began to grow in his belly, filling him with a fear such as he had never known before.

He licked his dry lips, licked them again. "What do you want to know?" he said in a voice that was not steady.

"Why," Johnny said, "just a few simple little things. Like who sent you after me with that gun? A contract, you'd probably call it. Little things like that."

Artie shook his head stubbornly.

"You're afraid of what might happen to you if you talk?" Johnny said. He shook his head. "You've got your priorities wrong, big man with gold chains. What you'd better think about is what *will* happen to you if you don't." He paused to let the words sink in. "If I walk out of here, with your gun and without you, you're already dead. And I won't even look back."

Artie took a deep, unsteady breath. "Even if I talk—" he began.

"You'll deny it all later?" Johnny said, and nodded. "Of course you will. And I won't care a damn. It's not you I'm after, it's who's behind you. And I'll get him, or them. Just the way I got you here. You can believe that, too."

9

The two cars drove back into town at a slow, steady pace. Artie led in the blue sedan, despite the air-conditioning still sweating, but now from more than heat, from fear he could not control. He was very conscious of the car behind him, and of the man in it with the rifle Artie had no doubt he would use without the slightest hesitation if the blue sedan attempted a getaway.

He remembered vividly what the cop had said as he picked up Artie's handgun with a handkerchief and tucked it in his belt almost contemptuously, all the while the other hand held the rifle unwaveringly pointed straight at Artie's belly.

"Standard form of suicide in these parts," the cop had said in that cold voice, "and has been ever since guns were invented—a handgun against a rifle. I could have blasted you a dozen times while you stumbled around in the rocks not even knowing what you were looking for. You may have been quite something back where you know the ground rules, but out here you're just dog meat. You might remember that."

Artie was remembering. And sweating as he drove. Without hesitation he turned in at police headquarters, parked, switched off the car's engine, and got out.

Johnny stepped out of the pickup and gestured with the rifle. "Inside," he said, and followed Artie through the doors and down the hallway to the desk where Tony Lopez waited. Tony was smiling cheerfully.

"Book him," Johnny said, and held out the handgun, still wrapped in the handkerchief. "Carrying a concealed weapon." To Artie he added, "Out here, that's a no-no."

Tony's eyebrows rose. "Just that?" he said. *"Nada más,* nothing more?"

"Why," Johnny said, "he hasn't done anything that I know of except get himself lost in some rocks like any big-city dude is liable to do."

Tony opened his mouth and closed it again in silence. Slowly he nodded. *"Entendido,* understood," he said, and the cheerful smile returned.

"I'll see you in my office," Johnny said in Spanish, and turned away, the rifle still in his hand.

He was at his desk, the rifle leaning against the wall, when Tony walked in and leaned comfortably against the wall to ask his question. "He talked?" Tony said.

"He talked," Johnny said with a faint nod. "He didn't think much of the idea of frying in the sun beside a disabled car while the vultures circled around waiting for him to die." He paused. "Which is what would have happened if I'd left him."

And the Indian would have gone off and left him, too, Tony thought, without even looking back. Unbelievable, but true. "I can't say I blame him."

"He'll deny it all, of course," Johnny said. "And even if I had it on tape, which I don't, it wouldn't mean anything because any judge would throw it out as inadmissable evidence. A man will say just about anything with a rifle pointed at his belly." He shrugged. "Besides, all he knows is that he was sent out to do away with a nuisance, me, who was bothering somebody."

"Bascomb?"

Johnny nodded again. "Bascomb it is. So now we know what we pretty well suspected all along. But we don't have any proof. And we don't even know what we're looking for, do we?"

Tony said thoughtfully, "An armor-plated car, and connections somewhere—Miami?" He watched Johnny nod for the third time. "Somebody," Tony said, "who's able and willing to send a hit man out here to give Bascomb a hand." He shook his head. *"Muy* damn *poco,"* he said.

Johnny nodded yet a fourth time. "We never had any guarantee that somebody would draw us a picture," he said, "so we assemble the bits and pieces as best we can." He was thinking with hope of little Mollie Higgins, her anger, her obvious intelligence, and her determination.

"Call it," Lucille Harrington said, "a committee meeting to see where we stand." She looked around the pleasant living room of hers and Waldo's house at Cassie, Mollie Higgins, and Waldo himself. "Agreed?"

"I'm out of place," Cassie said. "Numbers are not my thing."

"No, you're not," Lucille said quietly. "You are just as deductive as the rest of us, perhaps more. Mollie, you have the floor."

"There is nothing in Walter's papers," Mollie said, "to give us any clue to the numbers. Walter didn't keep a journal, or even notes, except in his head."

"Pity," Waldo said.

"And the film that was in his camera," Mollie said, "is just snapshots. Mostly of people." She colored visibly. "Some of them are of me. At my apartment near the university."

Cassie said thoughtfully, "We take photographs of digs because sometimes the backgrounds are important. Does that mean anything?" She looked around at them all.

"It very well could," Lucille said in that quiet, assured voice of hers. "Are there recognizable backgrounds in the photos, Mollie? Aside from those of you, that is?"

"Probably of Miami," Mollie said. "Walter spent some time there. There are palm trees, and buildings that look like they would be in tropical or subtropical climates." She shook her head helplessly. "Nothing that looks significant to me. Here." She dug into her bag and produced color photos to pass around and be studied in silence.

Cassie said, "There is something running around in my mind, something you told me about your husband, but I can't think what it was."

Mollie said almost apologetically, "He was secretive. And stubborn." She smiled shyly. "He disliked mathematics, numbers, theoretical reasoning. Concepts like the square root of minus one annoyed him because they contradicted themselves, and he thought the binary system was nonsense."

Lucille said, "A moment. The binary system? How would that have come up, Mollie?"

Again the apologetic smile. "When I was teaching

him to use the PC I almost forced him into buying, he—" She stopped. "Oh," she said, "how silly of me. I didn't even think of it."

Waldo said, "He had a personal computer? Where is it now?"

"I have it," Mollie said. "It was with the rest of his things."

"Mollie dear," Lucille said gently, "don't you think you had better ask it what, if anything, 12-22-88 means?"

"I am *so* sorry," Mollie said. "I *hate* being stupid!"

That night in front of the piñon fire with Johnny, Chico at their feet, Cassie said musingly, "I've been thinking. About what you said the other night— armored cars, guns, almost casual violence." She turned to look at Johnny's face in question.

"It all happens, *chica.*" He had not told her of his confrontation with Artie Gilmore and did not intend to.

"You said what it all suggested to you was drugs, wasn't that it?"

"It was. It is. But I can't make it fit. True, we had some problems here a while back."

Cassie shivered. "I remember."

"But there's no pattern. We're off the beaten path. Down in the city, the DEA is kept busy trying to stop the flow. But up here—" Johnny shrugged.

"DEA?"

"Drug Enforcement Agency. Justice Department. Feds."

Cassie stared thoughtfully at the fire. " 'Stop the flow,' " she said. "From where to where?"

"Mostly up from Mexico. Headed for California, L.A." Johnny took his turn staring at the flames as if the thoughts he was seeking could be found there. "That is big business, *chica,* big bucks, big city traffic. And we're a backwater." He was silent again. "Still," he said at last, "it's worth asking a few questions." He smiled suddenly. "You have a knack of making me see what's right under my nose."

Warm praise. Cassie savored it.

And so in the morning, both annoyed and astonished by the volume of commuter traffic he encountered, Johnny drove down to the city again and sought out the local DEA head, whose name was Howard.

"I guess what I'm asking," Johnny said, "is if there's any indication that up in Santo Cristo we're in the drug traffic pipeline?"

"None that I know of," Howard said. He seemed faintly amused. "Down here we have our hands full, but I think we'd hear of anything going on up your way—if there was anything."

Johnny could smile. "I know. We're a backwater, too hard to get to. It would be a detour up and then back down again. Makes no sense."

Howard was no longer amused. "Still, you're wondering," he said. "Mind telling me why?"

"Maybe," Johnny said, "because I'm grasping at straws. I hate to keep saying I don't know, but that's exactly how it is." He stood up. "Thanks, anyway."

"Anytime," Howard said, and stared thoughtfully at Johnny's back as he walked out. Ortiz, Howard was thinking; the name was not wholly unknown. A while back, a Santo Cristo police lieutenant named Ortiz had been mentioned in reports, and Santo Cristo, for all its publicity as a tourist and arts center, did occasionally have its share of action. Something to keep in mind, he decided, even though, as Ortiz had said, a detour up and back down again, a round trip of 130 or so miles, made no sense for drug traffickers who for obvious reasons wanted the shortest possible distance between two points.

From Howard's office, Johnny went to the Federal Building where Gus Goddard, the federal magistrate, held forth. The judge was available.

They shook hands. "Frankly," Johnny said as he sat down, "I don't know why I'm here. I know the answers to my questions all too well, and if I don't like the answers, as I don't, that's tough."

"I'm listening," Goddard said.

Johnny told of his encounter with Artie Gilmore, and their conversation.

"And," Goddard said, smiling a little, "where did all this take place?"

Johnny told him, and the judge whistled silently. "You led him all the way out there?"

"It seemed a good place to talk."

"I'm sure it was." The judge leaned back in his chair and turned his smile on the ceiling. "A man, and particularly a city man used to people and telephones, civilization, if you can call it that—he would have hell's own time making his way back from there if, say, his car broke down, wouldn't he?"

"The thought occurred to him," Johnny said. He did not mention that he had suggested it.

"And the odds that he would make it," the judge said, "are exactly zilch." He waved one hand. "I won't ask for particulars. At the moment they're unimportant. He's denying everything, of course?"

"Naturally."

"Are you going to file charges?"

Johnny shook his head. "We have him on a concealed weapon charge. And he isn't the one we want, anyway. He's just a hit man." His voice was carefully expressionless.

The judge took his time. "I think I'm reading your mind," he said at last. "You're going to use him as bait?"

"It may be interesting to see what happens."

"Interesting for you," the judge said, "but maybe fatal for him." He shook his head gently. "He might better have stayed out in the rocks with the ravens and the vultures."

Johnny shrugged. *"No importa,"* he said.

The judge was still leaning back in his chair, and again looked at the ceiling. "So now," he said, "we pretty well know what Higgins, the FBI man, was poking around for, no?"

"We know *who* he was interested in," Johnny said, "but we haven't any idea why. Which is right where we began."

The judge said, "Are you, like Higgins, going to ask for a search warrant?"

Johnny shook his head. "Would I get it? The answer is no. And even if I did, what good would it do? Bascomb is out in the open, a pillar of the community, entertains the mayor and the congressman and all the good folks. What would I be likely to find? Nothing."

"I must say," the judge said, "you have an interesting puzzle to solve, don't you?" He paused. "Think you can work it out?"

"Yes," Johnny said, and there was that in his face and in his eyes that underlined the statement. "If it takes until hell freezes over."

"Somehow," the judge said, "I believe you. If I can be of help . . ."

"Thanks," Johnny said. "I'll holler."

He drove back to Santo Cristo in a somber mood, thinking of Leon Bascomb, who was rapidly becoming something of a fixation. That break-in at Mollie Higgins's house, Johnny thought—Bascomb? Probably he was behind it, because what would little Mollie Smith Higgins have in her possession that might interest a professional thief except something related to Walter Higgins, FBI agent, deceased?

But Bascomb didn't wear boots, and the man who had left the tracks did. So what did that prove except what Johnny already knew, that Bascomb would be unlikely to get *his* hands or *his* feet dirty at little Mollie Higgins's house when all he had to do was send someone, as he had sent Artie Gilmore?

Back to Artie Gilmore. Was he known to the Miami police? Possibly, maybe even probably. It would be worth a query, even though whatever answer came back would still not connect Artie with Bascomb if, as was certain, both men denied any connection.

No, the problem was how to flush Bascomb into the open, in effect make him unmask himself—and how could that be done when he, Johnny, didn't even know what Bascomb was up to in Santo Cristo? What came inanely to mind was the ridiculous, unanswerable question medieval churchmen, as Johnny understood it, had once asked themselves with great seriousness: How many angels could dance on the head of a pin?

What he needed, Johnny told himself, was something to take his mind off the problem and in that way let it cleanse itself of improbabilities and misconceptions. And that, of course, meant Cassie.

As he came over the top of La Bajada hill and was in line-of-sight of Santo Cristo, he plucked the microphone from its hook and called headquarters for Tony Lopez.

"Check with Miami police," he told Tony, "a Captain Vasquez, and ask him if Artie Gilmore is known to them."

"Entendido," Tony said. "And then?"

"Call Cassie Enright at the museum and tell her I'll pick her up in ten, fifteen minutes. We're going for a walk in the mountains."

There was a smile in Tony's voice as he said, *"Servidor de tú,* at thy service. Over and out."

Cassie and Chico were waiting in front of the museum when Johnny drove up. As he leaned across the seat to open the door, he heard a wolf whistle that came from a group of young, male *turistas,* and he could smile, thinking that Cassie, even in wheat-colored jeans, a short-sleeved shirt and boots, fully deserved the implied admiration. He felt better already as Cassie got in and closed the door, and Chico sprang over the tailgate into the pickup's bed, his waving tail and protruding pink tongue showing his delight.

"We'll stop by the house," Johnny said, "and pick up jackets. It will be chilly."

Cassie was smiling fondly. "Where?"

Johnny shook his head helplessly. "Once again, *chica,* I find myself saying I don't know." And then, suddenly, "Yes, I do, at that. We're going to walk Elk Ridge, which is where it all began." He turned to look at her. "Okay?"

Her smile was his answer.

They left the pickup at the end of the Elk Mountain road. "Six miles along the ridge," Johnny said, "and six miles back. About five hours." He had the rifle in his hand, and a water bottle at his belt. "Agreed?"

"Let's go," Cassie said, and set off along the trail.

To their left, across the deep Pecos Valley, the rear of the Sangre de Cristo Mountains rose sharp against the limitless sky, snow from last winter still lingering in their folds and fissures. To their right, the land fell away endlessly.

"Lovely, lovely country," Cassie said. She walked easily and well, her rounded buttocks moving rhythmically. Chico ranged far and wide, his tail aloft and waving happily. "Are we searching for something?" Cassie said.

"No, *chica*. Just—" Johnny hesitated. "—absorbing the peace and the quiet."

"The rifle?"

"Pure habit, nothing more."

"I heard," Cassie said, "of a man named Gilmore, and a confrontation." It was a statement, no question, but it demanded an answer.

"Where did you hear?" Johnny said, although he might have guessed that word would spread. It always did.

"Maria Gonzalez at the museum is one of Tony's *primas*, cousins."

"Then all is explained."

"You are not angry?" Cassie spoke without looking around, walking at her steady pace.

Johnny thought of Judge Goddard and his guess that Artie Gilmore, loose, could be the goat tethered to attract the tiger. "On the contrary," he said, "a little publicity will do no harm."

Cassie walked for a time in silence. Then, "He was sent to kill you?"

"That was the general idea."

"Why?"

"I can only guess, *chica.*"

"That is no answer."

"Maybe I am getting too close to someone, even if I don't know how."

"Leon?"

"That would seem to be it."

"Do you want to talk about it?"

"No." Johnny hesitated. "For the present I'd like to forget all about it. Then maybe when I come back to it, I'll be able to see it with different eyes."

He was a strange man, Cassie thought, as single-minded as anyone she had ever known, and yet, as now, able to push his problems aside. With her help, she thought, and found pleasure in the concept. "Look," she said suddenly, "a hawk?"

"A golden eagle, *chica,* the great one. In his element, the sky, seeing far better than we can, soaring far better than any sailplane or hang glider, afraid of nothing."

"You sound envious."

"Aren't you?"

Cassie's eyes were on the great bird, broad wings spread and motionless, riding the wind currents without effort. "In a way," she said. "But I prefer it the way it is."

"*Yo también,* I, too, to be honest."

A mile or so farther on, Cassie said suddenly, "Listen!" A small, buglelike sound from the talus slope below. "What is that?"

Johnny smiled. "A pika, rock rabbit, singing his song to the neighbors."

"Isn't he afraid of the eagle?"

"He's safe," Johnny said. "Probably under an overhanging rock on his front porch. He'll have his hay spread out to dry, and when it *is* dry he'll store it for his winter nest, and his winter feed."

"All things arranged," Cassie said, and wondered where the thought had come from.

Johnny thought of Walter Higgins's shattered body down on the talus slope. "Until man disturbs them," he said, and they walked on in silence.

It was a trifle under five hours when they reached the pickup on the return walk. "Tired?" Johnny said.

Cassie shook her head, showing her lovely smile. "Refreshed."

Johnny nodded. *"Yo también.* It was just what I needed." He hesitated, but the words came out easily enough. "Thank you, *chica*. For everything."

Artie Gilmore was brought before County Judge
Benito C. de Baca, pled *nolo contendere* to the charge
of carrying a concealed weapon, and was fined and
released after an admonition from His Honor.

On his way out of police headquarters after getting
back the possessions he had surrendered when
booked, he encountered large Tony Lopez wearing his
cheerful smile. "Have a nice day," Tony said pleasant-
ly, and added, "Come back and see us sometime."

Artie decided that stony silence was the prudent
course, and walked out to the rented car without a
word, drove as far as the nearest public telephone, and
placed a call to Leon Bascomb's big house.

It was answered by a voice he did not recognize that
told him to hold on, and, after a brief pause, delivered
the following message: "Mr. Bascomb says he doesn't
know anybody by that name." The phone went dead.

Artie hung up slowly, and in something of a daze
walked back to his car. He got in and just sat, both
hands resting on the wheel, trying to accustom himself
to this new state of affairs.

He was unused to failure, and what was apparently

failure's inevitable result had never even occurred to him before. How far would Bascomb's reaction reach? There was the question, and he disliked the only answers he could think of.

Word, of course, would go immediately to Miami, if it had not already gone, and what would await Artie there would not be a simple telephone rejection. It would be cold, unforgiving anger, and the mere thought of it was unnerving.

The basic problem was that the humiliation he had suffered at the hands of that hicktown cop had badly shaken his confidence. Closing his eyes, he could still see those great, heat-radiating, red rocks, and the infinite space, a vast, unbarred prison from which there could be no escape.

He could also see the cop's face, and the rifle pointing at his belly, and see in the cop's stonelike eyes the certainty that the man, without hesitation, pity, or the slightest qualm, would do as he said, condemn Artie to a slow and horrible death in this alien land. It was then that something inside Artie had begun to shrivel, leaving him no longer the man he once had been.

So what to do now? That was the question, and he heard in his mind no answer.

Leon Bascomb was not happy. First there was the bungled attempt to retrieve Higgins's wristwatch, which Jorge ought to have taken from the body in the first place, and find out what the numbers engraved on its back were.

Maybe they were nothing, some date, perhaps, that meant something to Higgins, if not to his estranged wife. But somehow Bascomb didn't think so, and it was obvious that little Mollie Higgins didn't either.

And the more he thought about that, the less he liked it.

It hadn't taken much effort to find out about her, that she was a mathematician and computer whiz and was going to work up at the Lab as soon as her security clearance came through.

But what was more important was that she had, in effect, braced Bascomb at the gallery opening, almost throwing her suspicions in his face, and that he liked even less. An educated man himself, he had a healthy respect for Ph.D.s, especially in science and mathematics, fields beyond his ken, and he had an uneasy feeling that Mollie Higgins might know more than she had appeared to know about Walter Higgins's work and aims.

So? So that brought Bascomb to the second matter that was making him unhappy—Artie Gilmore's obvious failure in regard to the cop Ortiz. Bascomb knew no particulars, except that Artie, meek as a lamb, had driven in to police headquarters and given himself up—and that was as un-Artie-like behavior as Bascomb could imagine. What the hell had happened, anyway?

When Artie, released, had called Bascomb's house and asked to speak to him, Bascomb's response had been automatic—he certainly wanted no connection established that could link him in any way to what had to have been an attempt, although a thoroughly bungled attempt, on a cop's life. Now he was having second thoughts, because Artie was the only one who could tell him what had happened. And where was Artie?

First things first, Bascomb told himself. The Higgins woman was the more urgent matter, and he,

Bascomb, had damned well better decide what he was going to do about her.

Johnny sat at his desk and considered the fax report from Captain Vasquez in Miami concerning Artie Gilmore, alias two or three other names. A hit man, considered good at his job, frequently suspected, twice arrested and then released for lack of evidence, apparently a freelance gun with no *known* connections with identifiable underworld figures.

"So," Johnny said, "we are no farther along than we were."

Tony Lopez, leaning against the wall, said, "He mentioned no names in your little talk, *amigo?*"

"A man named Smith," Johnny said, "who probably, no, almost certainly doesn't exist."

"Gilmore," Tony said, "has not left town. He made one telephone call, a short one, then sat in his car for a long time probably thinking about it and finally went to El Rancho motel and took a room. *Es interesante, no?*"

"Good," Johnny said. "Then we'll be able to know what phone calls he makes—except for local ones."

"It could also be," Tony said, "that he decided, or was told, to stay around and finish the job he came out here for." He paused, and the cheerful smile was conspicuous by its absence. "Had you thought of that?"

"A possibility," Johnny said, "but I don't think it's worth a lot of worry. He's a marked man now, and he knows it." He was silent, thoughtful. "On the other hand, perhaps he's no longer after me, but after somebody else?"

"Who?"

Johnny's face was suddenly harsh. "Mollie Higgins has made waves." He told of her approaching Bascomb at the art opening. "She wanted him to think she knew more than she does, and maybe he believed it." He pushed back his chair and stood up. "I think a little talk with Bascomb is in order."

Tony pushed himself away from the wall. "I will go with you."

"No." Johnny's voice was definite. "He and I will talk alone. No witnesses." He thought for a moment. "Call him and tell him I will meet him at the same spot where he met Gilmore."

Tony looked doubtful.

"And then call Ben Hart," Johnny said, "and tell him, too."

Tony's cheerful smile appeared as he considered the implications. *"Muy bueno.* And *el oso pardo,* the grizzly bear, will be watching. With rifle?"

"Something like that," Johnny said. "Ben enjoys being involved."

The 30-30 carbine was again in the rack across the window of Johnny's pickup in plain view. Johnny drove slowly, setting his thoughts in order, deciding just how far he could logically go with Bascomb in conversation. When the radio call came from Tony saying that Bascomb was on his way to the rendezvous, Johnny said merely, *"Bueno,"* and hung up the microphone.

The gray Cadillac was already stopped on the lonely side road when Johnny arrived. As Johnny got out and walked over to the big car, the near window slid down and Bascomb, his face expressionless, said, "What is the meaning of this? I am not used to being summoned."

"But you came," Johnny said. "So we'll talk. Away

112

from your car. This conversation is just between us, without tape recorder."

The tinted window rose smoothly, and after a moment Bascomb opened the door and stepped out, in his short-sleeved shirt obviously unarmed and carrying no tape recorder. Johnny noted the sound the door made as Bascomb closed it, and thought that Charlie Cottrell had been entirely right; it did sound like a door closing on a safe.

"Well?" Bascomb said. "Get to it. It's hot here in the sun."

"Gilmore found it hot, too," Johnny said. "He was lathered up like a cutting horse by the time we finished talking."

"Who is Gilmore?"

"The man you sent to kill me." Johnny's voice was matter-of-fact. "There's no point in denying it. I said he talked. About quite a few things." He paused. "You would never have seen him alive again if he hadn't talked."

Bascomb blinked. "You would have killed him? Whoever he was?"

"I wouldn't have touched him," Johnny said. "I would just have fixed his rented car so it wouldn't run and left him there to die. He *might* have lasted through the day. You can believe that. He did."

Bascomb was silent for long moments. He said at last, "What do you want?"

"You." Johnny paused again. "And I'll get you, too. It may take time, but I'm patient."

"Is that a threat, Lieutenant?"

"No. A promise. You can believe that, too. In the meantime . . ."

"Yes, Lieutenant?"

"In the meantime, if anything happens to Mollie

Higgins, if anybody breaks into her house again, I will probably run out of patience and come after you. You can believe that, too."

"On what charge, Lieutenant?"

"I may not even have one," Johnny said. "I may just deal with you the way I dealt with Gilmore. Only you won't come back." He looked up. "See that bird? It's a vulture." The large bird rode the air currents, rocking on its dihedral wings. "By the time it and its friends are finished with you, there won't be anything but clean bones."

"There are laws, Lieutenant."

Johnny nodded. "So there are. But you flout them, and I can, too."

"You wouldn't dare."

Johnny smiled. It was not a pleasant smile. "Try me."

There was a silence that grew, and stretched. Bascomb said at last, "Was that all, Lieutenant?"

"For now. I suggest you remember what I said." And then, as if in afterthought, "Oh, by the way. You claim not to know Gilmore. But all Tony told you was to meet me where you had met him. And here you are, aren't you? Think about it, Mr. Bascomb. Think hard. And if you want to reach Gilmore, he's at El Rancho motel."

Bascomb turned away without a word and walked back to the gray Cadillac. Again the sound of the door closing reminded Johnny of a door closing on a safe, or a vault. The Cadillac's rear wheels spun as Bascomb drove away.

When the Cadillac was out of sight, trailing its dust plume, Ben Hart appeared on the other side of the fence. Ben was on horseback, and a saddle gun, a

30-30 carbine, rested in its scabbard beneath his right thigh. "Have a nice chat?" he said.

"Not exactly a heart-to-heart," Johnny said, "but I think he got the message."

Ben leaned on the swell fork of his saddle in a contemplative manner. "Man like that," he said, "sometimes has more tricks than a coyote. Mark Hawley says the record shows Bascomb don't care much for women." He paused. "But that don't mean he couldn't use them—if he found it handy, now does it?"

"Meaning what?" Johnny said.

"That filly of yours," Ben said. "She works for the museum. And Bascomb sits on the museum board, no? Man in his position can throw his weight around quite considerable if he wants to." He paused again. "Come to that, a man like him can call in help to do his dirty work, just like he did with that feller Gilmore. And much as I like your filly, I don't think she's up to coping the way you did with somebody who means her harm."

"If anybody even tries to mess with Cassie—" Johnny began.

"Just something to think about, son," Ben said. He straightened in the saddle and waved one big hand in a friendly farewell gesture. *"Hasta luego,"* he said. "I can lend a hand, let me know."

Johnny watched the old man's broad back as he rode away at an easy running walk. Cassie, he told himself, was indeed something to think about. Old Ben Hart had seen that more clearly than he had.

Mollie Higgins sat in front of Walter's personal computer, watched it go through its warm-up checks, and waited until the blinking signal indicated that the machine was ready for business.

With the ease of long experience, her eyes on the screen as her fingers moved swiftly, she typed 12-22-88, watched the figures appear, and waited for a reaction. There was none.

Mollie smiled and spoke to the computer as to a person. "Wrong question?" she said. "Or just plain reluctance?" Her fingers moved swiftly again, repeating the query. Again no reaction. "Wrong question," she said, and leaned back in her chair to think while the computer waited patiently.

Walter was, had been (it was still difficult to think of him in the past tense) an intelligent man, and, as she had said in the Harringtons' living room, both stubborn and secretive as well. *Secretive,* was that the operative characteristic?

Logic, she told herself sternly; logic is your business, is it not? Then apply it. Would Walter, a secretive man, have had openly engraved on his watch an important series of numbers *exactly* as they were meant to be applied?

If he had, then the number series was meaningless to the computer. But if he had not? Well, what if the numbers were correct, but they were not in their correct sequence? Mollie sighed deeply.

For six numbers there were—she worked it out in her head—720 different sequences possible, less the duplicates caused by the two sets of identical numbers. Would Walter have trusted himself to remember which of the hundreds of possible sequences was the one he intended to remind himself of, or, more likely, to pass along to her, Mollie, if he met with an accident? It seemed illogical; if the numbers did indeed have significance for the computer, Walter would have chosen a far simpler arrangement, would he not?

Her fingers flew as she typed the numbers in exact reverse order: 88-22-21. The computer remained adamantly unresponsive.

She blanked out that sequence and punched in instead: 88-22-12. Again no response, and again she cleared the screen.

Think, she told herself, *think!* The numbers were in groups of two digits each, three sets. With three sets, there were only six possible combinations, no? And she had already given the machine two of them. So try the other four: 12-88-22; 22-12-88; 22-88-12, and 88-12-22.

It was on the third of the remaining four sequences, 22-88-12, that the computer paused, and then, to Mollie's mind as if it were heaving a great sigh and saying to itself, "At last!," began to flash words on its previously blank screen.

At the weekly Rotary Club meeting, Charlie Cottrell, Joe Todd, and a man named Bud Brookings, head of the local IBM office, sat at the same table.

"How's business?" Charlie Cottrell said. "It's great. Folks are getting tired of those expensive foreign luxury cars and are turning back to the good old USA products. My Cadillacs are selling to beat the band. Mostly cash deals, too. There's money around, lots of it."

"My business has picked up too," Joe Todd said. "Seems everybody and their brother are moving west, California, Arizona, getting out of those eastern winters."

Brookings said, "You've got your parts inventory on computer, Charlie, but have you ever thought of computerizing your customers and their preferences, their car checkups, and maybe even personal things like birthdays, anniversaries? And how about you, Joe, don't you have some repeat business, or wouldn't you like to see exactly how many communities you service and how you can best allocate your equipment or project allocation over the coming year, that kind of thing?"

"Sounds to me," Charlie said, "like IBM is scratching pretty hard for business. Are you hurting, Bud?" He was smiling as he asked the question.

"Big blue is doing just fine, thanks," Brookings said. "But, seriously, how about it, you two? Suppose I send someone around to see what we could do to help your business? No obligation, of course."

Joe Todd said, "I don't really see the point. I send out shipments, make deliveries, and that's an end to it." He smiled. "Unless we get complaints, which isn't very damn often. One thing I make plain to my people is be careful and handle all shipments like they were your own."

"I think, Joe," Brookings said, "no offense meant, that you could maybe perk up your operation some if you give us a chance to do an analysis. Some time back you weren't being quite so upbeat, so maybe we could help you a bit more. I'll send a man around. Just talk to him, okay? Let him see what he can figure out."

The IBM man Bud Brookings sent around to Todd Van & Storage was named Talbot, and he was bright, brushed-up, and neatly, even carefully dressed in a dark suit in accordance with IBM tradition. "If it's okay with you," he told Joe Todd, "I'll just poke around a bit here in your office." He smiled. "Trucks and vans aren't my thing, so there's not much point in my going into your garage layout. Not yet."

"Oh, hell," Joe Todd said, "help yourself. Jennie here can give you whatever you want to see."

They met again as Talbot was going out to lunch. "Interesting, your operation," Talbot said, and shook his head in mild wonder. "I didn't know there *were* that many little towns and places in Arizona and southern California."

"Big area," Joe Todd said, "and we know it pretty well."

They met again at the end of the day. "I have a couple of ideas I'll work up," Talbot said. "Mostly they have to do with your routings and schedules to make them easier to call up and make promised delivery times and dates." He smiled, again in mild wonder. "You've got a couple places, one in Arizona, one in California, I didn't know were that big. Must have wonderful climate, the way people are moving to them."

"I spent a winter in the East once," Joe Todd said, "and that was enough for me. Cold, damp, gray, you felt like you were living in some kind of purgatory." He paused thoughtfully. "Way I figure it, these partloads, these aren't rich folks like used to come west for the winter. These are little people, without too much furniture, ordinary people just fed up with where they're living."

"A lot of them," Talbot said, "from Texas, down Galveston way, and from along the Gulf Coast."

"I hadn't really noticed," Joe Todd said. "I've been too busy." He was to think of that later.

11

Leon Bascomb drove back to his big house after his talk with Johnny in a thoughtful, and unhappy, mood. Like Artie Gilmore, Bascomb was unused to failure, and it suddenly seemed that his impregnable world was beginning to crumble around him—all because of a small-town cop.

That the cop obviously had no proof that would stand judicial scrutiny was small comfort. The goddamn Indian—Bascomb rarely used profanity even in his thoughts—the goddamn Indian *knew* of the connection between Artie and himself, so obviously, as the cop had claimed, Artie *had* talked.

Worse, there was growing in Bascomb's mind a sneaking admiration for the cop. That bit about refusing to talk with Bascomb while Bascomb was still in his car was smart. No tape recorder, as Johnny had said, no witnesses to testify that, yes, Lieutenant Ortiz *had* threatened Bascomb openly.

And that sneaky bit about having the sergeant telephone and merely say that Johnny would meet him, Bascomb, at the place where he had met the other man, not even mentioning Gilmore by name. The sergeant had been smooth; he had sneaked that one past too fast for careful examination.

The plain fact was that this town of Santo Cristo, with its history and its art and its reputation as a place where money liked to retire, belied its lazy, laid-back appearance. Aside from Johnny Ortiz and his obviously tricky sergeant, there were others, Will Carston, Cassie Enright, the Higgins woman, even old Ben Hart the rancher and Congressman Hawley, who were too smart for their own good, too nosy. And he, Leon Bascomb, was beginning to feel as if he were standing naked and alone on stage in the full glare of the spotlight.

He stopped the Cadillac at the gate outside his property and lowered his window enough for the guard to identify him, open the gate, and wave him through. That was the one disadvantage to these heavily tinted windows; from the outside you couldn't really tell who was driving the car. Or how many people were in it. More food for thought as he drove up to the big house.

Jorge, summoned, stood in the paneled study waiting for instructions.

"Artie Gilmore," Bascomb said. "You knew him in Miami?"

"To recognize him, *sí.*" Jorge nodded.

"He is staying at El Rancho motel." Bascomb hesitated, but his mind was made up, and he went on. "I want you to give him a message."

Jorge waited.

"Just two words," Bascomb said. " 'Get lost.' " His face changed subtly. "Add one more: 'Fast!' *Entendido?*"

"Sí, señor." Jorge was smiling.

"That is all," Bascomb said. Artie, having botched his assignment, could fend for himself—but somewhere other than Santo Cristo.

When the door had closed after Jorge, Bascomb put the matter of Artie from his mind and settled down to some hard thinking. Ortiz, Mollie Higgins, yes, and Cassie Enright, too, these were the key players, the first two because they represented a threat, and the third because she might provide the leverage to pry at least that goddamn Indian Ortiz off the trail. *Bueno.* Now for ways and means. . . .

Words on a computer screen were one thing, but words on paper were far better, more permanent. Mollie Higgins hooked Walter's computer to her own printer and ran off two copies of all the information contained in file 22-88-12. One copy she sealed in an envelope, and left the house carrying it in her bag.

She walked to the museum, where she found Cassie in her office, Chico beneath the desk. "I find," Mollie said in her apologetic way, "that I have to go away for a few days. Perhaps you won't mind keeping this for me while I'm gone?" She laid the sealed envelope on Cassie's desk.

Cassie looked at the envelope and then at Mollie. "And I am to open it if you—don't return?" She paused. "What are you up to?" she said.

"It's—personal."

"I hate to say it," Cassie said, "but I'm afraid I don't believe you, Mollie. Your husband's computer told you something?"

"Only hints."

"Which are in here, and which you intend to follow up?"

"Someone has to."

Cassie shook her head. "Johnny—"

"Walter was *my* husband." The shyness and diffidence disappeared all at once as if wiped away. "I have an obligation."

"For revenge?"

"No," Mollie said. "I don't think it is that exactly." She paused. "It is rather that I would not like to think that Walter died for—nothing. He left me a message. I am convinced of that."

"The numbers on the watch?"

"Exactly. He would have known that sooner or later I would understand what they meant, and—" The shy smile reappeared. "—do *something* about them, or find someone who would do something about them."

"Which brings us right back to Johnny," Cassie said.

"No." The shyness was again gone. "He is a policeman. His place is here in, if I may say so, his own environment. I am free to visit other places."

The woman, Cassie was thinking, was a bewildering blend of timidity and a determined strength worthy of Johnny himself, and it was difficult, if not downright impossible, to keep up with the sudden switches between the two attitudes. "Mollie," she said, "these, whatever they are, are hardly matters for—"

"A woman to deal with?" Mollie said, and shook her head vehemently.

Cassie smiled gently. "No," she said, "that is not what I was going to say. Women can be every bit as capable as men, but in their own fields. And this is not your field, is it?"

Mollie was silent, but her chin remained stubbornly set.

Cassie tried once more. "Will you talk with Johnny?"

"No. That is why I came to you. You can explain to him how I feel."

Cassie said, "I'm not even sure I know. Just how *do* you feel?"

"In a word," Mollie said, "angry. And if you won't keep this for me—"

"Oh," Cassie said, "I'll keep it. How could I refuse?"

Once again the shy smile appeared. "Thank you," Mollie said. "Thank you very much."

Cassie threw up her hands and shook her head in bewilderment and helplessness. "I know now," she said, smiling, "why men sometimes say you cannot argue with a woman." The smile disappeared. "But," she said, "I will make one condition, Mollie. If I keep this envelope for you, will you promise to telephone me every day and tell me you are all right?"

The shy smile remained intact. "All along, I intended to," Mollie said.

That evening in front of the fire, "So there it is," Cassie said. "I tried, but I couldn't stop her."

"Has she already gone?" Johnny said.

"Yes."

"Do you know where?"

"No. But she will call me tomorrow." Cassie hesitated. "I'm worried about her, Johnny. She is such a strange little person."

"I could be wrong, *chica,* but I have an idea little-desert-pocket-mouse Mollie Higgins will be able to take care of herself."

* * *

Tony Lopez said, "There is an *hombre* named Jorge Trujillo. I hear things about him." It was the next morning, and Tony was leaning against the wall in Johnny's office.

"Go on," Johnny said.

"He is a helicopter pilot," Tony said. "For a time he flew for the potash people, ferrying brass from the office out to the mines and back."

"And now?"

"He flies for Bascomb and keeps the Cadillac and the chopper in shape." Tony was silent for a moment. "He also went to see Gilmore at the motel." He paused again.

Johnny sat silent, waiting.

"Gilmore packed up and left," Tony said. "So maybe Trujillo carried a message?"

Johnny thought about it, and nodded. "Likely. Bascomb wants him out of Santo Cristo. Do we know where he went?"

"Miami."

"Did he make a phone call first? The motel records would show."

"No phone call. He just left."

"Then," Johnny said, "I think we'd better plug Captain Vasquez in."

"Claro." Tony's smile was broad and cheerful. "Is already done."

Johnny permitted himself a tight little smile of approval. "And Trujillo?" he said. "What of him? That he flies Bascomb's chopper is interesting, *sí*, but what does it prove? That he dropped a corpse on Elk Ridge?"

"He came here from Miami," Tony said. "About two years ago. He was originally *Cubano.*"

Johnny thought about it. "Everything seems to point to Miami, no?" he said.

"Sí." Tony shrugged hugely and spread his hands. "Beyond that, I cannot go."

Again the tight smile appeared. "If it makes you feel any better," Johnny said, "that makes two of us. Higgins was from Miami, a gang member there before his father yanked him out to Michigan. Bascomb is from Miami, with a Cuban father." He paused thoughtfully. "What about his mother? Who was she?"

The mind of the *brujo*, Tony was thinking, scurried busily like a *cucaracha*, a cockroach, from point to point as if it smelled morsels of food invisible to the naked eye. "I suppose he had one," he said. "Most people do, *amigo*."

Johnny's face was still thoughtful. "Ask Captain Vasquez if he will be good enough to find out about her," he said, and for the third time the smile appeared. "No, I do not know what I am after. All I have is a vague hunch that demands scratching."

Tony's face expressed resignation. *"Servidor de tú,"* he said, and walked out.

Johnny sat quietly for a time, staring at the wall. Then, as if unable to bear inactivity any longer, he pushed back his chair and walked out past the front desk. To Tony he said, "I am going for a walk."

Tony smiled. "Understood." And he added, "Some of the female *turistas* who walk about the Plaza are worth studying. They seem to wear less clothing each year."

"You belong on a vice squad," Johnny said as he walked out.

He had no destination; the physical exercise of

126

walking was an end in itself, opening his mind from the confinement of four walls. He passed the cathedral with its asymmetrical towers, and the compound that had once belonged to General Sena, who, it was said, had added a new room for each new child until the enclosure was complete.

Johnny reached the Plaza and circled it once at his steady pace. Tony, he thought with a smile, had been quite right: There were many female *turistas,* frequently strolling in pairs, and it was evident from their bouncing breasts that they wore less clothing than had once been the style. But none of them held a candle to Cassie, and his interest in them was ephemeral.

Something was running around the edges of his mind and he could not isolate it, which was annoying, but he knew that the only solution was patience, and he made himself think of other things.

Miami. He had never been there, and had no desire to go. He had been to Las Vegas, the one in Nevada, not the one in New Mexico, which he also knew; and he imagined that it and Miami had much in common —perhaps a sense of artificiality? And both, of course, had reputations for illegal activities.

He was not a moralist, as such. Most of the questionable indulgences common to our society were, in his opinion, purely personal matters to be settled by each individual according to his own conscience.

But certain activities affected society as a whole, innocent and guilty alike, and these he refused to accept or condone. Murder, as in the case of Walter Higgins; any and all overt brutality; theft of another's possessions; wanton destruction of property; and above all, wanton destruction of *people,* as in drug trafficking—these he found unforgivable, and he was prepared to oppose them by almost any means.

It was in this contemplative frame of mind that he found himself entering the museum and heading, as a beaver to water, straight for Cassie's office.

She was in, smiling, and lovely as ever. That this miracle had happened to him, Johnny thought as he had so often before, was beyond comprehension.

"Hi, *chica,*" he said. "Not busy, I hope? I am playing truant and trying hard to think." He shook his head. "About what, I do not know." He sat down and studied Cassie's face. "There is something on your mind."

"Mollie called me." Cassie's happy smile held. "I was sure she would. And she is quite all right, she says, which is a relief to know."

"Did she say where she is?"

"Yes. Miami."

Johnny closed his eyes. Where else? All roads and threads led to Miami, no?

It was then, as if on cue, that the telephone rang on Cassie's desk. She picked it up, spoke her name, listened, and held it out to Johnny. "For you. Tony Lopez."

Tony's voice was quiet and filled with wonder. He said, "You saw visions, *amigo?* There is no other explanation. And Captain Vasquez had seen them, too. He was about to call us when I called him."

"I'm listening," Johnny said. And it was then that what had been running around in his mind came out into view. Of course, of course. What Higgins had said about Bascomb not being the name the man was born with.

"Bascomb's mother," Tony said, "was divorced. Bascomb was her second husband. She already had a son. Named Lee. When Bascomb formally adopted the boy, the name was changed to Leon."

Johnny blinked. "That is all?" It could not be, he thought, there was more. He was sure of it, although he could not have said why.

"No." Tony's voice had taken on a different, more incredulous note. It was as if he were speaking of a miracle beyond belief. "There were two sons of the first marriage. The other one went with the father."

"Out to Michigan," Johnny said. At last it was clear. "His name was Walter, no? Walter Higgins?"

Tony's voice clearly expressed his sudden sense of deflation. *"Exactamente.* You spoil my ending. Walter Higgins and Leon Bascomb were brothers. Cain and Abel, no?"

Johnny hung up the phone and looked at Cassie. "You heard?" He watched her nod. "There is said to be a snake," he said, "that takes its tail in its mouth and rolls like a hoop. I am beginning to think that this Bascomb-Higgins business is doing precisely that. It seems to have no real beginning, no reason, and no end that I can see."

"But you will find it," Cassie said. There was deep conviction in her voice. She smiled gently. "Because you will not give up until you do." *Implacable* was the word, she thought, but did not say aloud.

Bascomb had another telephone call from Miami, and the same crisp, authoritative voice speaking English said, "Artie's back. He do what you wanted out there?"

"No," Bascomb said, and found it hard to keep the anger he felt out of his voice. "He blew it. A local cop booby-trapped him and I think scared the shit out of him in the bargain."

There was a noticeable pause. The voice said at last, "That's how it is, is it?" Another pause. "Okay. Another thing. There's a little schoolteacher type in town asking questions. Name of Smith, Mollie Smith. Know anything about her?"

Bascomb said carefully, "I've met her." He hesitated, and then, because it would all come out anyway, he added, "Her last name is Higgins. She was married to a guy who got himself dead. An FBI guy."

"That," the voice said slowly, "doesn't sound very good. You know what I mean?"

"It's all under control," Bascomb said.

"Sure about that?"

"I told you, under control."

There was another pause. "Okay," the voice said. "We'll leave it like that. Business is good?"

"Couldn't be better."

"How about this local cop? He under control, too?"

"Everything is copacetic."

"Why is this dame asking questions?"

"I don't know, but *no importa.*"

"Sure about that? Maybe we'd better suggest she ask questions someplace else."

Tempting, Bascomb thought, but unwise. "She can't do any harm." What did that damn wristwatch say, anyway? What were the numbers and what did they mean?

The voice said, "You're a real smart fellow, Leon, but just don't screw up, you know what I mean?"

"Exactly."

"Okay," the voice said. "Let's keep it copacetic, like you said."

Bascomb hung up and sat quiet, scowling at the wall. Why was Mollie Higgins in Miami? And why was she asking questions? About what? Maybe Cassie Enright would know. Bascomb had heard that she and the Higgins woman had become real friendly. So.

He called the museum and asked for Cassie. "Will you have lunch with me again? I have something I would like to discuss." Better make it good, he told himself. "It concerns a gift I am thinking of making to the museum, and I would like your opinion."

That night, "How could I refuse?" Cassie said. "Even if he is—whatever he is, a gift is a gift is a gift, and all museums always need money." She studied Johnny's face. "What are you thinking?"

Johnny stared at the piñon flames. "It's just that maybe, just maybe, he's beginning to flounder a little. It's starting to sound like it."

"Should I go?" Cassie said. "I told him I would, but I could always back out."

"By no means, *chica.* At the Palace, in the open, you're perfectly safe. Let's see what he's up to."

"I'm not good at this kind of thing," Cassie said. "I don't dissemble well."

"You'll do just fine, *chica,* just fine. Think of the gift, and see what else he has to say, that's all." Johnny's voice took on a note of caution. "Let him do the talking. Don't you ask questions of your own." He patted her thigh. *"Entendido?"*

Cassie nodded. "Understood."

Mollie's voice on the telephone the next morning was a trifle breathless. "I'm still in Miami," she said, "but I'm going down to the islands. A piece of luck."

"Tell me," Cassie said.

"Well, it occurred to me," Mollie said in the shy, self-deprecating voice, "that a travel agent here in the area might recognize the backgrounds in the pictures from Walter's camera."

Cassie smiled. "Good thinking. And one did?"

"Yes. Bahamas and Grand Cayman."

"You'll call me?"

"I will indeed. I'm getting quite excited. It's like— doing research!"

12

As before, Leon Bascomb was waiting in a booth at the restaurant when Cassie came in. He rose politely and remained standing until she was seated. Then, smiling, he seated himself.

"I watched your entrance," he said. "I don't think there was a male eye in the house that was not turned in your direction."

"There are not many blacks in Santo Cristo," Cassie said easily, "so I am used to being stared at."

"Are you afraid of compliments?"

Cassie could smile then. "No. I enjoy them, as most people do—if they are sincere."

The waiter appeared, and Cassie ordered a glass of white wine.

"Then do you find me insincere?" Bascomb said when the waiter was out of earshot.

"I'm not sure," Cassie said truthfully. "Are you? With some it is hard to tell."

Bascomb watched the waiter bring Cassie's wine and put it before her. He acknowledged the service with a faint nod. "I am afraid," he said slowly, again when the waiter was out of earshot, "that your thinking is colored by your friend Lieutenant Ortiz. He takes a dim view of me, as I believe you are aware."

"Johnny and I make up our own minds," Cassie said. "There is that tacit understanding between us." She was smiling as she raised her glass. *"Salud,"* she said.

She felt, not ill at ease, but keyed-up, every faculty alert as if in an important contest the aim of which was to discover an elusive truth and examine it carefully. She was to let him do the talking, Johnny had said, and to ask no questions herself. She would try to follow instructions.

Bascomb said, "You do not subscribe to the lieutenant's view that I am a criminal, then?" He was smiling easily. "I can assure you that I don't have cloven hooves or a tail."

Cassie could smile, too. "Speaking as an anthropologist," she said, "I doubt if anyone has or ever did have. All religions have their myths."

Bascomb was silent for a few moments. "I mentioned a gift," he said at last. "Perhaps we had better talk about that. Ten thousand dollars is not a vast sum, but I imagine it could be useful. You agree?"

Cassie shook her head wonderingly. "As far as I am concerned, ten thousand dollars is a great deal of money, and, yes, it could be very useful."

"To your work?"

"Of course, but that would be up to the board to decide."

"Not," Bascomb said, "if I earmarked the gift for your particular use."

Cassie thought about it. "I am not sure I could accept that," she said at last. "There are jealousies, probably in every organization, and I would rather not run the risk of offending others unnecessarily."

"Is that your only reason?"

"What else?" Cassie watched the man steadily. "Unless, of course, the gift had strings attached."

"No strings."

"Then I think the best procedure would be to make the gift through channels."

"You don't trust me, do you?" Bascomb said, and again the easy smile was in evidence. "Neither does your little friend—Mrs. Higgins, isn't it? How is she, by the way?"

"I haven't seen her in a few days," Cassie said. "I think she may have gone back to Michigan to tidy up her affairs before she starts work up at the Lab." The lie came easily enough.

I am discovering how devious I can be, she thought, and felt a tinge of shame. She could almost see Johnny's smile if she told him how she felt. He takes a more realistic view of humanity than I do, she told herself, perhaps because he has to deal with it as it is, not, as I do, concentrating on and trying to reconstruct the past.

"She approached me at a gallery opening," Bascomb said, "and seemed to hint that I had had something to do with her husband's death. Did you know that?"

"It is hardly the kind of thing she would tell me," Cassie said. "I didn't even know her husband."

Bascomb sipped his drink and set it down slowly. "I have the feeling," he said, "that we are almost sparring with each other. I am sorry you feel as you do. I should like us to be friends." He smiled suddenly. "Shall we order?"

"He sounded sincere," Cassie told Johnny that night.

"But what, *chica?*"

"He pretended," Cassie said, "that he wasn't even sure of Mollie's last name." She shook her head slowly. "And the dead man was his *brother?*" Her tone was incredulous.

Johnny shrugged. "Tony mentioned Cain and Abel. The comparison is apt, no? But we have no proof." His tone was angry.

"There must be something!"

Johnny shrugged again. "Maybe. Maybe not. The good guys don't always win."

"He sent a man to kill you!"

"That was the general idea."

"Why?"

Johnny took his time. "Spell that one out, *chica.*"

"You can't prove it," Cassie said. "I understand that. But isn't it proof enough for you to—point a direction? Guns, violence, get-in-my-way-and-I'll-waste-you, you said it yourself."

"Drugs, you mean?" Johnny nodded. "I'd almost bet on it. But it makes no sense. Not up here, out of the mainstream."

Cassie closed her eyes. When she opened them again, her expression had changed. She said now in a voice that was filled with conviction, "Chaco Canyon."

"What about it?"

"I have flown over it," Cassie said. "It, what is left of it, sits out there in the middle of nothing, all by itself!"

Johnny said slowly, "Go on."

"But even now," Cassie said, "after hundreds of years, you can still see the trails, roads that led to it like spokes in a wheel. They come from almost every

136

point of the compass—north, south, east, *and* west.
How and why did it get to be such a center?"

"You tell me, *chica.*"

Cassie shook her head. "We don't know. Not for
sure. But the fact is evident that it *was* a hub. And it
had to have been started for some reason by someone!"

Johnny was shaking his head slowly in wonder.
"Beautiful," he said, *"and* oh, so bright, too. You are
quite a package, *chica,* quite a package."

He was up and dressed at sunup the next morning,
leaving a warm bed, and Cassie, with only scant
explanation. "I have some thinking to do," he said as
he went out.

There was no traffic, and in the silent, deserted
streets the traffic lights seemed, and were, out of place;
civilization demonstrating its frequent futility, Johnny thought, as he headed as if drawn by a magnet for
the great mountains that look down upon Santo
Cristo.

The ski basin road, too, was empty, as he had hoped
it would be. He drove its narrow, climbing turns
steadily, without haste, his destination firmly in mind.

In the early, cool morning the scent of pines was
plain, refreshing, the forest on either side of the road
unspoiled. Up one of the small draws down which an
intermittent stream flowed cautiously, a deer, drinking, threw up its head, ears alert, as the pickup went
past. From the road itself, three ravens rose without
panic from their feast of what remained of a dead
rabbit and, wings flapping noisily, hovered overhead
until they could safely settle down again. In a small
clearing, Johnny caught a glimpse of gray and white,

probably a Clark's nutcracker, as it took flight and disappeared.

Here he could breathe deeply of clean air free of automobile exhausts and other man-made pollutants, and it seemed that his mind itself could expand and think more easily and more deeply, pursuing the thoughts that Cassie had stirred into action the night before.

The totality of Chaco Canyon, as Cassie had implied, was best seen from the air, the Pueblo Bonito ruins and those of the ancillary structures, the network of ancient roads well traveled long before Columbus, a center dating back a thousand years, its cause and purpose still unclear.

Here, where he pulled off the road at the 10,000-foot level, 3,000 feet above the city, he could also look down as if from an aircraft and view Santo Cristo in its totality. He switched off the engine and got out to walk to the edge of the drop-off for his long, thoughtful look. His view was unobstructed from northwest to almost due south.

There was the interstate, in this area running almost straight north-south, with almost no traffic showing as it climbed gradually to the south and then dropped over La Bajada grade. In the distance the bulk of Mount Taylor, more than 100 miles away, rose sharply on the horizon; and in the nearer foreground was the irregular mass of the great caldera, on the slope of which Los Alamos seemed to cling precariously.

Immediately beneath him was Santo Cristo itself, the low-lying houses dotting the hills and collecting into masses closer to the center of town, their colors ranging from near-white to dark-brown adobe, a few of their chimneys showing smoke.

The city *was* isolated, almost surrounded by mountains, with no immediate east-west passage possible. Think, he told himself, *think!* Why here? What possible reason could Leon Bascomb have had in mind when he moved lock, stock, and barrel from Miami to Santo Cristo? Because there had to be a reason, and Walter Higgins must have known or guessed it—and died as a result. There was no other logical explanation.

A movement caught his eye, and he studied it and made out the diesel locomotive on the spur track that led to Santo Cristo from the transcontinental railroad track at Lamy, seventeen miles to the south-south-west. And as he looked at the locomotive and the three cars it pulled, the sound of the diesel horn came clearly in the morning air, stirring a thought in his mind, quickly gone before he could examine it.

How long he stood at the edge of the drop-off and the talus slope beneath it, looking out at the still-sleeping city, he was never to know. But at last he turned away, disappointed, and walked back to the pickup to start the return drive. There were four ravens at the dead rabbit to rise at his approach, but he saw no deer and no nutcracker, no other wildlife as he descended into town. A single jogger, female, trotted through the red light at which he stopped briefly, but that was all.

When Tony Lopez came in that morning, Johnny was already at his desk, staring at the far wall, seemingly oblivious. But when Tony started to withdraw, Johnny said, "Come in. Close the door. Sit down and listen." Tony obeyed without comment.

"You know Chaco Canyon?" Johnny said without explanation.

"*Sí.* I have been there. Why, I do not know. Out in the middle of nowhere."

"Exactly." Johnny's voice was sharper than usual. "Why was it there, a center? What was its attraction?"

Tony shrugged hugely and spread his hands. "You tell me, *amigo.*"

"There had to be a reason."

Another shrug. *"Probablemente."*

"If it became a center, as it did," Johnny said, "for reasons we don't really know, then why couldn't Santo Cristo, well off the beaten track, also become a center where a man named Bascomb chose to live?"

Tony blinked, thought of a quip, and decided not to make it. Instead, "The Chamber of Commerce says we *are* a center, *amigo,*" he pointed out. "That is why the *turistas* come in such numbers."

Johnny nodded. "Art, tradition, the opera, chamber music—do you think these are the reasons Bascomb came here?"

Tony thought about it. "Maybe yes, maybe no. I do not know."

"Neither do I," Johnny said, "but I doubt it."

"What then?"

The locomotive horn sounded again. Probably at the Cerrillos grade crossing on its return trip, Johnny thought, and all at once he began to see what he had been searching for. He could even smile.

Tony, watching the smile, said, *"Qué pasa?"*

Johnny said, "Bulk transportation. That's what trains are for, isn't it?"

"Claro. So?"

"So I have an idea," Johnny said, rising from his chair. "Maybe a wild one, but at least a place to start."

Tony closed his eyes. He said, "You are seeing visions in smoke again?" He shook his head.

"Maybe," Johnny said. "We'll just have to see."

"Bueno," Tony said in a tone of resignation. "I will wait."

Howard, the local DEA head, was again in his office down in the city when Johnny arrived. "I have some silly questions to ask," Johnny said. "I hope you have time for them."

Howard smiled faintly. He had looked up the federal file on Lieutenant Ortiz, and silly questions did not appear. "Shoot," he said.

"Dope," Johnny said, "heroin, cocaine, whatever you have to cope with, how does it travel?"

Howard smiled again, sadly this time. "You name it. Boat, car, aircraft, either private or commercial, for all I know in motorcycle saddlebags or tourist box lunches. We've found it in thermos bottles, in brassieres, in money belts and attaché cases—" He spread his hands. "It travels any way those who want it and those who sell it can figure out."

"We found it once in pieces of Mexican sculpture," Johnny said.

"I know about that. Just one more way." Howard paused and shook his head angrily. "What we do know," he said, "is that the hell of a lot more is getting through than we manage to stop. How, we don't know." He studied Johnny's face. "You have ideas?"

"So far that's all they are, purely hypothetical."

"If they turn out to be more than that," Howard said, "we'd like to know about them."

"You will. That's a promise."

From Howard's office, Johnny went again to the Federal Building to see Judge Goddard. "How much probable cause do we need for a federal search warrant?" he said.

"That strictly depends," Goddard said. "Care to tell me what you have in mind?"

"So far only a guess," Johnny said. "It goes like this."

The judge listened quietly and with interest, and when Johnny was finished he nodded. "Smart," he said. "Damn smart. You develop it, and come back here with a few facts, and we'll see about a warrant. We might even stretch a point if we have to."

Johnny stood up. *"Grácias."*

"De nada." The judge, too, was standing. He held out his hand. "Good luck," he said. "Or, better yet, good hunting."

Johnny drove back to Santo Cristo in a thoughtful mood. Coming up with an idea, even one that looked and sounded good, was one thing. Implementing it in all of its possible ramifications was quite another. Although he hated to admit it, the task was too much for a local cop all by himself. For what he had in mind, Mark Hawley was the answer.

Congressman Hawley, his secretary said, was out at Ben Hart's ranch and, yes, she would call there and tell them that Johnny was on his way.

It was eight dusty miles from Ben Hart's cattle guard to the main ranch house, built of stone like a fortress but with huge picture windows to admit views of the great mountains surrounding the area.

It was, as Cassie had once remarked, a blend of Ben's memories of earlier days when a man's home damn well had to be his defensible castle, and his love of the country and his knowledge that in present times a man could afford large areas of glass. "Something like Ben himself," Cassie had said. "He and Mark Hawley fit into today's world, but in a sense they are still throwbacks to a time when a man had to depend on himself."

There were Indian rugs of price on the polished brick floor of the huge living room, and the gun cabinet against the wall was not for show, containing as it did shotguns, rifles, and handguns and, in the locked drawers, boxes of ammunition for all.

"You got a burr under your saddle?" Ben said as Johnny walked in. "You got that scalping look in your eye. Set and tell us about it."

Johnny sat down. "It was Cassie's mention of Chaco Canyon that started me thinking in this direction," he said, and went over the ground he had covered with Magistrate Goddard.

When he was finished, "Whoosh!" Ben Hart said. "When you think big, you think big!"

Mark Hawley was silent, turning the entire matter over in his mind. "You're pointing in a lot of directions, son," he said at last, "but it does make sense. You want help from Washington? Yep, I can see that. Things have to be, like they say, coordinated."

"Man's swinging a wide loop," Ben said, "damn wide."

"It's got to be," Mark Hawley said. "Unless you got a better idea?"

Ben heaved himself out of his chair. "I do. Let's have a drink and talk about it."

13

Mollie Higgins's voice on the phone was filled with enthusiasm. "It's so lovely down here," she told Cassie. "The water is a color, or I should say many colors, that I have never seen before. And warm! I've even been for a swim!" She paused, and her voice turned shy again. "Not," she said, "that I am much of a swimmer, or even very decorative in a swimsuit. It's just that I couldn't resist." The last sentence was almost an apology.

Cassie stifled a smile. "And just where are you?"

"In the Bahamas. And the tourist lady was right about the picture backgrounds. I've located two of them. They are banks. Tomorrow I go to Grand Cayman."

Cassie said, smiling no longer, "Have you been talking to people? Asking questions?"

It was the shy voice again. "A few."

"Remember," Cassie said, "I don't even know what you're looking for, but if your husband was interested in it, it could be—not exactly guaranteed safe, Mollie. You are remembering that?"

"All I have to do," Mollie said apologetically, "is

find one particular bank account. That doesn't sound very difficult. Or in any way dangerous, if that was what you meant."

"That was exactly what I meant," Cassie said. "I think you'd better have . . . official help. Maybe Johnny can arrange it."

"This," Mollie said firmly, "is *my* research. I will call you tomorrow." Her voice altered as she pleaded for understanding. "Please, Cassie."

Cassie sighed and made a face at the wall. "I'll wait for your call," she said.

Talbot, the IBM man assigned to Todd Van & Storage, said, "I've set up a rather simple program showing points of origin, sizes of loads, frequencies, destinations, times of travel—that kind of thing."

Joe Todd stared doubtfully at the computer Talbot had set up on his desk. "These things scare the hell out of me," he said.

"It's user-friendly."

"You mean it won't bite?"

"It won't even scold you," Talbot said. "Look. Suppose you want to see what destinations you've shipped to in, say, California, and what the exact loads were and the dates. Okay?"

"I suppose so."

"All you do is push this button. When the query comes up—see?—you just type in CA for California. Simple. Like this." Talbot touched two keys.

Instantly the screen of the computer came alive, and a neat row of letters and figures appeared, then another and another until the screen was filled. "See?" Talbot said. "Now, if you want to continue, we call it scrolling, you just push this button."

"Wait a minute," Joe Todd said. He was staring at the screen. "How are these arranged?"

"Alphabetically, although we could use any sequence you prefer. We—"

"Hold it," Joe Todd said. "You said you have points of origin listed, too?"

"Easy. We erase this and call up 'origin.' I've given it a code of five. Press the five button."

Joe Todd pressed the button gingerly. Another neat row of letters and figures appeared, and another until the screen was again filled.

"Now," Talbot said, "if you want—"

"Just leave it be," Todd said. "I want to look at it."

Talbot smiled. "That's simple, too. Let's print it out, then you can study it all you want. Okay?"

Todd nodded. "I'd like to see that," he said.

"Nothing simpler. You'll be surprised how fast the printer prints."

The phone call for Johnny came just after eight o'clock in the morning. The voice of Captain Vasquez, Miami police, said, "I'd have called earlier, but there's some kind of time difference, isn't there? I didn't know how much, and I hope I'm not too early now."

"Two hours," Johnny said. "But that's fine. I'm down early. What's up?"

"You remember Artie Gilmore?"

"Quite well."

Captain Vasquez's voice was matter-of-fact. "They fished what's left of him out of the water early this morning. Thought you might like to know."

Nothing changed in Johnny's face. "Thanks, Captain."

"Word is," the captain said, "that something must have happened to him out there in your territory, because when he came back he wasn't the same tough *hombre* he had been." He paused. "And a hit man who's scared of his own shadow isn't much use, in fact could turn out to be a liability."

"Is that what happened?" Johnny said, his face still unchanged.

"That's how it figures," the captain said. "No big loss." He paused. "On the other hand, mind telling me what did happen out there?"

"Nothing much," Johnny said. "He just learned a few facts of life out west."

There was another pause. "I see," the captain said. "You mean, the way Custer did?"

Tony Lopez, leaning against the wall, saw the shadow of a smile lift Johnny's lips. "Something like that," Johnny said. "We have our own ground rules, Captain, just as you do."

There was a smile now in the captain's voice. "I ever come out there," he said, "I'll ask you to explain those ground rules to me first."

"Will do," Johnny said. "Thanks for the call."

"Anytime."

Johnny hung up and looked at Tony Lopez. "Scratch Artie Gilmore," he said.

Tony nodded understandingly. "He was dead when you brought him in, *amigo*. He just hadn't figured it out yet."

There were a number of banks on Grand Cayman, Mollie Higgins discovered, and it was not until she reached the fourth that she hit pay dirt.

She walked in, small, shy, smiling her apologetic smile, and asked to see the manager.

The young man at the desk was distantly polite. "May I ask the nature of your business, madam?"

"Why," Mollie said, "it is, uh, personal." She shook her head. "No, it is not exactly that, really. It's just that it concerns my husband's business, and he told me to insist on speaking to the manager." She smiled helplessly. "He was quite definite," she added, "and he would scold me if I didn't do as he says."

The young man hesitated, stood up, and nodded. "A moment, Mrs.—?"

Mollie smiled. "I don't really believe my name is all that important, but if you like, you may call me Mrs. Smith."

"I see," the young man said vaguely, and turned away. He was back in only a few moments. "This way, please, Mrs. Smith." He showed her into the inner office, where an older, gray-haired man sat behind a large desk. The door to the office closed discreetly.

"What may I do for you, Mrs. Smith?" the manager said. His manner was distant, too.

Mollie's voice took on a firmer tone. "I should like to know the balance of my account," she said, and took a piece of paper from her bag and laid it on the desk. On it was written: 88-22-12.

The manager looked at the paper. He looked at Mollie with a different, less formal expression. He cleared his throat. "Is that—all, madam?" he said.

Mollie's apologetic smile appeared. "How silly of me! Of course!" She dug into her bag again and took out another piece of paper with a single word on it: *Washington.* "I confuse easily," she said. "I mean, numbers and complicated things like that are always difficult for me."

The manager was already standing. He picked up the two pieces of paper and held them out to Mollie as if they were contaminated.

"I keep them separate," Mollie said. "I mean, one without the other is meaningless, isn't that true? That is what my husband told me."

The manager smiled faintly and nodded. "Quite so, madam," he said. "I approve of your prudence. Please make yourself comfortable. I shan't be a moment." Again the door closed discreetly.

Mollie stuffed the two pieces of paper back into her bag, and then just sat, and made herself breathe deeply while she waited. When she heard the door behind her open again and shut quietly, she put on her shy smile, but did not turn.

The manager walked around to his chair behind his desk. He held out a paper. His tone, if not quite obsequious, was hushed. "This is the current balance in the account, madam," he said. "Would you also wish a complete breakdown of the figures?"

"Dear me, no," Mollie said. "As I told you, numbers tend to confuse me." She glanced at the paper he had handed her, blinked once, smiled, and said, "But this seems quite clear." She rose and held out her hand. "Thank you, Mr.—?"

"Russell," the manager said. He, too, was standing, and he took Mollie's hand gingerly and bent over it with a small bow. "Would you—ah—like some funds, Mrs. Smith?" he said.

"Thank you, no. I have ample for the present."

Mr. Russell watched Mollie tuck the paper in her bag. "If there is any way I can be of service," he said, "please do not hesitate to let me know."

"So kind," Mollie said, and hesitated, smiling the shy smile. "There *is* one thing, Mr. Russell," she said in her diffident voice. "If I am not being too difficult, that is."

"Anything, madam, anything at all."

Mollie told him what she wanted.

She left Grand Cayman that afternoon and returned to Miami, where she took a flight to New York the next morning. She called Cassie from New York's La Guardia Airport and told her where she was. She added, "I think I am being followed." She paused. "In fact, I am quite sure of it. I am speaking from a public telephone in the United Airlines complex near Gate 14."

Cassie was thinking hard. "Then," she said, "stay right there and I'll see what I can do." Johnny, of course.

"No," Mollie said, and her voice was quite definite. "I have given it considerable thought, and I think it will be best if I just faint." She dropped the phone and collapsed into a small, helpless huddle on the floor.

Cassie heard loud voices talking in confusion. And then the phone went dead as someone apparently hung it up. Cassie disconnected, too, and dialed Johnny's number in desperate haste. She felt an enormous sense of relief when he answered. "It's Mollie and she's in New York and being followed . . ." The words almost ran together.

There was even a hint of a smile in Johnny's voice when he said, "She thought it best to faint? Smart girl. I'll take it from here, *chica.* And relax. It's going to be all right."

He called Howard, DEA head down in the city, and rapidly explained the situation. "She," Johnny added, "is on her own, but she's trying to unravel part of the story, so in a sense she's working for me, us, and I feel responsible. She—"

"Done and done," Howard said. "You seem to have clout, Lieutenant. I have orders to cooperate with you." His voice held no particular resentment. "We'll take over."

Mollie, on the floor, eyes closed, heard the babel of voices and then a new voice, authoritative, saying, "Move back, please." And, in a change of tone, "Yes. Gate 14. Over and out." Again in the authoritative voice, "A stretcher is on the way. Move back, please."

There was a short wait. Mollie lay quite still. Then there were voices again, calm voices this time, and hands expertly lifted her and laid her gently on a firmly yielding surface. She felt herself being driven away with a wailing, warning sound presumably clearing a path down the crowded corridor.

She heard a door open and close, and then there was quiet. A hand checked her pulse, and after a moment a voice said, "Strong and steady. And her respiration's okay. We'll just let her rest a couple minutes. No sweat."

So far, so good, Mollie thought, and wondered what was going to happen next. She stifled the temptation to open her eyes and look around. Not yet, she told herself; it's too soon.

There was a knock on the door and the sound of someone coming in. "This the lady, doc?" a voice said.

"Yes. And she's okay. Who are you?"

"DEA. Feds. Here." There was a short silence, presumably for ID scrutiny. "And when she starts coming around, we'll want to talk to her. Alone. Okay?"

Mollie decided it was time to open her eyes. The first thing she saw was a large, solid man still holding a small leather case in his hand, the kind of leather identification case Walter had carried. Mollie blinked.

"You okay, lady?" It was the large, solid man speaking.

Mollie nodded. Her lips formed the word, "Yes," but she made no sound.

"Okay," the large man said to a man in white. "Just a few minutes." And when the door had closed and Mollie and the large man were alone, although Mollie felt another presence behind her, "A guy following you, that's it, Mrs. Higgins?"

Mollie found her voice. "Yes. A large, blond man with a short crew cut, unusual, isn't it, these days? He's wearing a poplin suit, tan, and a striped necktie."

The large man produced a broad grin. "The faint was a fake?" He nodded. "Smart. We'll take care of the guy. You got luggage?"

"I'm taking another flight. My luggage is being transferred."

"What flight? Time?" The large man looked at his watch. "You got plenty time. It'll be Gate 16. Just go on along when you're ready. Nobody'll follow you." He smiled. "You got guts, lady. And smarts."

"Why," Mollie said in the shy voice, "why, thank you. Thank you very much."

"Have a good flight," the large man said.

"And that," Howard the DEA man said on the phone to Johnny, "is how it was. They picked up the guy and turned him over to ATF."

"Momentito," Johnny said. "ATF? Sometimes your fed alphabet names are too much."

"Bureau of Alcohol, Tobacco, and Firearms," Howard translated. "They're Treasury, but we cooperate. There's a federal law against a convicted felon carrying a gun. Our boy had one, and he'd done time. He'll do some more now—without parole. Your little lady's coming in on American Flight 230 at just after ten tonight. Want her met?"

"We'll meet her, thanks."

"Way I hear it," Howard said, "the whole thing didn't even faze her."

"No," Johnny said, "it wouldn't." He hung up and stared at the wall. And I thought she was a desert pocket mouse, he told himself. You are not a good judge of females, Juan Felipe. He amended that: except for one. He called Cassie to report.

Mollie wore the shy smile when she came through the gate where Cassie and Johnny waited, but the smile was also tinged with triumph. In Johnny's pickup, Mollie sandwiched between Johnny and Cassie, "Did you find the bank account?" Cassie said.

Mollie's voice was very small, and her smile was apologetic, as if she feared she might be caught boasting. "Yes. On Grand Cayman."

Johnny said, "How and what and the rest can wait for a moment." His voice was commanding. "The man who followed you, who's now in fed custody, where did he pick you up?"

"In Miami."

"Then you went to the Bahamas?"

"Yes."

"Did he follow you there?"

"No."

"Sure?" Johnny's tone was solemn. "It's serious."

"I am sure," Mollie said. "I, uh, took evasive measures, if that is the phrase, and watched carefully. He did not follow me to the Bahamas. Nor was he on Grand Cayman. I watched carefully there, too."

"Good." Johnny's voice held relief. "Now, back to the bank account."

Mollie told of her eventual encounter with Mr. Russell. "He was a trifle formal. Walter's information was not quite clear, so I had the number and the code word on separate pieces of paper. It turned out that both were needed. After that, Mr. Russell was as cordial as could be. A very nice man, actually. When he gave me the balance, he asked if I wanted a complete breakdown. I said no."

"How on earth," Cassie said, "had your husband obtained the number and the code word of a secret bank account?"

"That, *chica*," Johnny said, "I don't think we'll ever know, unless it was in the information he left."

"It was not," Mollie said, "and I wondered myself how he could have had it." Her shy voice appeared again. "But does it really matter now?"

"It does not," Johnny said. "It is entirely *no importa*. You had it, and that's all that counts."

Cassie said, "Are you going to keep us in suspense? What was the balance your Mr. Russell gave you?"

Mollie said in her small voice, "You won't believe it. I don't myself, and I have read Mr. Russell's figure a dozen times." She took a deep breath, and then, spacing the figures for emphasis, said slowly, "The figure is $21,598,432.14!"

Cassie gasped. Johnny smiled at the road. "Well, well," he said. "No wonder your husband seemed excited. It's just a pity he kept it to himself."

Whatever it has picked, and it's loaded up.

Joe could get none of the drivers, at least the few still able to make a telephone call, to admit fatigue, an inability of a human being the size of a man to take so much, was nothing. A forty-eight-hour run was forty-eight-hours, and drivers said it like they said day's work. There was no bad humor. Joe Todd had once been scarred by a load himself and could understand it. But he was afraid. It was happening. He told him, all right, you can run a few hours but over...

14

Joe Todd studied the computer printout Talbot had run for him—places of origin and places of destination of part-loads he had been happily transshipping west to Arizona and California.

There was no doubt that the IBM computer monster was efficient. In addition to places, the times, weights, and dates, too, were all meticulously listed, all i's dotted and all t's crossed. And the volume of business was even greater than Joe Todd would have guessed. As he had told Talbot that first day, he had been too busy to pay much attention to just how much came from where, and where it was going. The profitable monthly statements had caught his eye, but not much else.

Now, scanning the folded sheets, their edges perforated, the neatly spaced holes seeming to give the printout even more authority, he was flabbergasted at what he saw.

There was a town he had not even heard of on the Texas coast from which folks seemed to be fleeing as fast as they could, judging from the volume of household goods that had come part-load to the Todd warehouse to be unloaded and then loaded again and sent on west.

There was also a town on the Mississippi coast that Joe had never heard of, either, and it, too, was apparently losing its population at a fearsome rate.

These, as Joe Todd had told Talbot, were not rich folks heading west for the winter to escape ferocious eastern climate. These, if what they shipped in boxes, barrels, and crates accompanied by stacked furniture and whatever else had escaped the presumed garage sale was any indication, were folks moving all their possessions to a new home out west. Probably they themselves drove, maybe even with a U-Haul trailer following the packed family car filled with kids and the dog.

Bascomb had certainly been right: Folks were moving west in droves. Joe Todd supposed the next census would show just how many had flowed into Arizona and California during the past decade, but he, Joe Todd, on the strength of this newfangled computer printout, could surely testify that the volume was damn near unbelievable. Not that he was complaining, mind you; those monthly sheets were pleasant reading indeed.

Howard, the DEA man, called Johnny from the city. "I'd like to come up for a talk," he said, "okay?"

"Whenever," Johnny said. "Be glad to see you."

With Howard came another man named Ogilvie. "From Washington," Howard said when he introduced him, "the upper reaches of the agency."

Ogilvie smiled at Johnny. "Your congressman knows the right people to call and the right arms to twist when he wants cooperation. No offense; the old boy usually has a good reason when he throws his weight around."

"Mark," Johnny said, "is pretty savvy." He paused. "But this time he threw you a curve?"

"Not exactly," Ogilvie said. "As I understand it, it was your idea, and it was a good one. Far more drugs get through than we are able to intercept, and that, as you reasoned, argues bulk transportation—maybe trains, as I understand was your original idea, maybe commercial aircraft, trucking, transcontinental buses, that kind of thing. All of those are suspect, and we do spot checks. But what we come up with is peanuts—somebody with half a dozen marijuana cigarettes, one or two fixes of heroin or coke, maybe a little crack." He shrugged. "Nothing that even begins to explain the volume of drug traffic there actually is."

"Through here?" Johnny said.

Ogilvie shook his head. "As Paul here told you, Santo Cristo isn't high on our list of hot spots. Albuquerque is because it's on a direct east-west route. Not quite the shortest route from El Paso and other Texas points along the Mexican border to California, L.A., San Diego—that's I-10 through Las Cruces, Deming, Lordsburg, and Tucson. But I-40 through Albuquerque is old Route 66, and it carries an awful lot of traffic through Flagstaff and on into California."

"Our airport?" Johnny said. "No commercial service, but a lot of private planes. And the man I'm looking at has his own chopper."

"That's Leon Bascomb?" Ogilvie said, and nodded. "We've had our eye on him for a long time." He spread his hands. "But we've never been able to pin a thing on him. Respectable businessman in Miami, ditto here." He paused. "Sorry. Nice try, but no cigar. But we wanted you and your congressman to know that we did follow up, and will continue."

"Thanks," Johnny said. "We can't win them all."

Ogilvie said, "If you don't mind my asking, what got you started thinking in this direction? Santo Cristo, I mean?"

"Chaco Canyon." Johnny explained about its being a center a thousand years ago out in the middle of nowhere.

Howard looked puzzled, but Ogilvie nodded. "And why not Santo Cristo with Bascomb here? That was your thinking?" He nodded. "Smart." He smiled sadly. "I only wish we could find a connection."

When they were gone, Johnny called Mark Hawley's office. "He's in Washington," his longtime secretary said. "Sorry."

Then the DEA would already have explained to him, Johnny thought as he hung up. He sat and stared at the wall. The diesel locomotive whistle sounded clearly, and Johnny turned a wry smile in its direction. He felt very much alone.

Bascomb had another phone call from Miami. The authoritative voice said, "Your phone isn't bugged or anything?"

"No." Bascomb's voice was definite. "I check it myself, and I know what I'm doing."

"I hope so. Because Joey Arnold's in the slammer facing a fed rap. He was following that schoolteacher type and the Feds picked him up after she fainted at the airport. Joey was carrying, and he's got a record, and that means five with no parole." The voice paused. "So who's the schoolteacher, and what does she know that brings in the Feds?"

Bascomb stared at the floor-to-ceiling bookcases. "I don't know."

"Then you'd better find out."

"Yes," Bascomb said, "I think I had."

"She wasn't in Miami the whole time."

"Where was she?"

"We don't know. Joey lost her for a couple days. She could have been anywhere."

"I'll look into it," Bascomb said.

"You do that, Leon. And look good, you know what I mean?" The voice paused. Then, with no change of expression, "By the way, Artie Gilmore got himself dead. He came back here, and something had scared him real bad, like you said. He ever got picked up, he'd never stop talking." The voice paused again. "Thought you might like to know." The phone went dead.

Bascomb hung up slowly. It was that cop, he thought, it had to be. Never mind Artie Gilmore; he knew what had happened there. But hadn't the cop warned him off Mollie Higgins? Her particularly? Why? What was the connection? Again Bascomb had the feeling that his impregnable world was beginning to crumble, and the worst of it was that he had no idea how, or why.

Mollie had lunch with Cassie. "I am quite excited," Mollie said, and smiled apologetically. "It's not very much, really. I mean, what is coming is not very much, but I have missed it. You know how you do?"

"Not exactly," Cassie said, smiling, "because I'm not really sure what you're talking about."

"Oh, dear. I've done it again, haven't I?" Mollie's expression was abject. "When things are so clear in my mind, I sometimes think other people understand, too. I am sorry. I'm talking about my things. From Michigan. The really very few things of my own I had in my apartment. There is a chair I love, and my own desk." She colored suddenly. "And the comforter Walter and I slept under while we were living together. Just small things, but, as I said, I miss them."

"Of course you do," Cassie said.

"The moving people have packed them up," Mollie said, "and they are coming, part-load, I think is the term. There isn't enough to fill a moving van. Walter and I didn't have very much."

That night, "Sometimes," Cassie told Johnny, "Mollie seems so forlorn, unworldly, even pathetic. I want to pat her on the head and tell her everything is all right." She paused. "What are you smiling about?"

"Poor little helpless Mollie Smith Higgins, *chica*. The desert pocket mouse frightened of her own shadow."

"Her things," Cassie said, "are coming part-load. She doesn't have enough to fill a moving van, she says, so she has had to wait until a van was filled."

It was in the middle of the night that Johnny came suddenly wide awake and sat up. At his side, Cassie said in a startled voice, "What is it? What's the matter?"

"*Estupido! Yo,* I, me, *cretino!* Of course, of course!"

"Now," Cassie said, "you sound exactly like Mollie. I don't have the faintest idea what you're talking about."

"Go back to sleep, *chica*. I'm going for a walk. I have thinking to do."

Bert Clancy was in his office at the bank the next morning, and Johnny was there when the doors opened. "I think this had better be private," Johnny said, and closed the door.

"Mysteriouser and mysteriouser," Bert Clancy said. He was smiling. "What's on your mind this bright morning? You want a loan?"

"Just talk," Johnny said. He took his time. "You told me once that you were considering Leon Bascomb as a member of your board, no?"

Bert was smiling no longer. He now wore his banker's face. "That is true," he said after consideration.

"Are you still thinking of him?"

"That," Bert said after a pause, "is, ah, official bank business."

"I'm sure it is. But are you?"

"Why do you ask?"

"Never mind that. Are you still considering him? This is just between us."

Bert thought about it. He said at last, "As a matter of fact, yes, we are. Now will you tell me why you ask?"

"Don't," Johnny said, and let the single word hang in the air.

Bert Clancy thought some more. "You can't leave it there," he said at last. "Give me reasons."

Johnny nodded. "I'll give you reasons. A swap. My information for some of yours. Just between us. A deal?"

Again Bert took his time, walking all around the offer as if examining it for booby traps. "That," he said, "is buying a pig in a poke."

"You won't think so," Johnny said, "when you hear what I have to say. And if you're satisfied, then you answer some of my questions in return. A deal?"

Bert took a deep breath. He inclined his head in the faintest of nods. "A deal," he said.

"So now just sit and listen," Johnny said.

Bert Clancy sat and listened, and his expression went from mild interest to mild skepticism to outright incredulity. "He sent a man to kill you?" he said. "Surely you are joking!"

"Fellow named Artie Gilmore," Johnny said. "Known to the Miami police as a hit man. He came after me with a gun, and he wasn't intending to show me what a pretty piece it was."

"But," Bert said, "but what happened?"

"He was fined," Johnny said, "for carrying a concealed weapon. Then he got a message from Bascomb telling him to get out of town, so he went back to Miami. They fished what was left of him out of the water the other morning."

Bert swallowed. "Dead?" His tone was incredulous.

"Very dead," Johnny said. "It's what tends to happen when professional hit men lose their touch." He paused. "And there is one other little item about Bascomb. He has an offshore numbered bank account with more than twenty million in it, and he didn't get that by saving Safeway coupons."

Bert had regained some of his composure. "Do you have proof of all this?"

"Enough. But I want more, and with your help I'll get it. We agreed on an information swap, remember?"

"Ah," Bert said, "naturally there are bank matters, confidential bank matters that I can't divulge. You understand that?"

"No," Johnny said, and his voice had taken on an edge. "You hold up your side of the bargain, or I spread the word that you have been and still are considering Leon Bascomb for your board of directors." He paused. "And when it all comes out, as it will, you will look like the biggest damn fool walking around loose." He paused again. "If you don't think I *would* set you up that way—try me."

For long moments Bert's eyes searched Johnny's face. He decided that he might as well be studying a stone statue, and not a very pretty one at that. "How do I know," he said slowly, "that any of what you have told me is true?"

"I'll let the implications of that go," Johnny said. "So pick up the phone and ask Mark Hawley. Or call Captain Vasquez of the Miami police. Or ask Ben Hart."

Bert swallowed again. He took a deep breath. "What is it you want to know?" he said. Capitulation.

Ten minutes later, Johnny got out of his chair and nodded. "Thanks," he said. He added, "This is just between us, remember? And if any of it leaks, I'll know where it came from. Understood?" He walked to the door then. "See you around, Bert," he said as he went out.

Back in his own office, Johnny summoned Tony Lopez. "Close the door," he said. And when it was closed and Tony was leaning comfortably against the wall, "You were born here in Santo Cristo," Johnny said, "and you're related to half the town. You have *primos* just about everywhere, *verdad?*"

Tony showed white teeth in a broad grin. *"Más o menos,"* he said.

"Bueno. I want you to put the arm on a *primo* to get me some information, without anybody knowing it, *anybody."*

"You are seeing visions, *amigo?*"

Johnny permitted himself his tight little smile. "Maybe. Maybe not. We'll see."

"Bueno," Tony said. "What information do you wish?" He spoke in Spanish and was grinning no longer.

Johnny told him, and Tony shook his head in wonder. "You are serious?"

"Completely."

Tony sighed. His expression was resigned. *"Servidor de tú,"* he said. "I will try." He hesitated. "Tell me, *amigo,* what kind of wood do you use to build the fire in which you see these visions in the smoke?"

"That," Johnny said with no hint of a smile, "is an ancient tribal secret."

Tony sighed again. "I was afraid of that," he said, and went out.

Mollie came to see Johnny that afternoon. She sat in his office, prim and meek and shyly apologetic as she had been that first day. "I hesitated about coming here," she said in her small voice.

"No need. The door's usually open."

"You are such a busy man. And my, ah, problems are so unimportant!"

Nothing showed in Johnny's face. "Suppose," he said gently, "that you tell me about your problems? How would that be?"

Mollie took a deep breath. "It's just—" she began, and there she stopped, then started over. "I think I am being followed," she said. And she added, "Again."

"It can't be the same man," Johnny said. "The Feds have him locked up."

Mollie shook her head. "This is a very different

man. Hispanic. He has black hair and he wears boots."

Boots, Johnny thought. They were not unusual here in Santo Cristo. Still . . . "Have you seen him before?"

Mollie produced her shy smile. "It's funny you should ask that, because I have the feeling that I have. But I can't remember where."

"Maybe in the dark? In your house? The man with the flashlight? Could he be the one?"

Mollie's face brightened. "It could be! I only got the impression of his movements, but this man does seem to remind me—of that night!"

Johnny pushed back the chair and stood up. *"Bueno.* We will find out. This is what I want you to do."

Mollie left police headquarters. Jorge Trujillo, watching from his car parked a little distance away, picked up his microphone and spoke into it. "She has left. On foot. Over."

"Follow her." The voice came immediately. "See where she goes now. Over and out."

Jorge got out of his car. He gave Mollie a head start and then began to follow her, staying always on the other side of the street. Such a small one, he thought, so like a small, frightened kitten; he wondered why she should be important enough to follow.

Of course, there had been the gun in her hand that night, no? He could smile now, thinking about it. She would never have used it, except perhaps in fright. She lacked the spirit, the *machismo;* you could tell just by looking at her as she walked now as if fearful that just by being there she might cause someone inconvenience.

She seemed to have a destination. *Bueno.* Jorge had nothing else to do and it was a nice day, not too hot, not at all like Miami or Havana where the heat was oppressive because of its dampness. This heat was light and the air was clear and dry, altogether pleasant. He walked at an easy pace, keeping his distance.

They reached the Plaza, swung partly around it, and there Mollie entered a large, carved door. A museum of some kind, Jorge thought, although he had never been inside. No matter. He found a convenient bench and sat in the cool shade of a tree while he waited. *Turistas* strolled past, some of them *chicas* in scant clothing, shorts and halter tops or, better, thin blouses beneath which Jorge could see their breasts jiggling as they walked.

El jefe, the boss, now, Señor Bascomb, he seemed to have no interest in women. Strange. If he, Jorge, had had only a tithe of the money Bascomb obviously had with his big house and his big car and the helicopter, why, the house would have been filled with girls, no? Yes. A pleasant thought to contemplate as he sat here relaxed in the cool shade and watched the *turistas* stroll by.

The little Higgins woman reappeared, looked around in her frightened way, and then set out once more. Jorge heaved himself up from his bench and followed.

Again the small woman appeared to have a destination, and as they walked it became apparent what it was. She was headed for her house, and in no hurry, because she stopped from time to time to look in the window of a gallery at paintings or pieces of bronze or maybe a brightly colored rug. From time to time, she glanced at her watch.

Jorge found himself wondering who the woman was

and why she seemed to be important to *el jefe*. She seemed so . . . *insignificant* was the word he had been searching for, so why in the name of *Dios could* she be important, especially to a man like *el jefe* who cared nothing for women?

They reached the woman's house. She turned into her dirt drive and walked steadily toward the door, where she got out her key and opened the lock that a child could have opened with a bent pin, and walked inside. It was only after the door had closed that Jorge started slowly up the drive.

He had gone perhaps twenty feet when behind him Johnny's voice said, *"Bueno.* Hold it right there. This is a rifle pointing at your spine. Put your hands behind your head."

It was the cop, Jorge thought, and wondered where he had come from. No matter. He was here, his voice unmistakable. And although Jorge had never spoken to him, he had heard much about him and did not like what he had heard. He raised his hands and clasped them behind his head.

"So," Johnny said, and with one hand searched Jorge's sides quickly. *"Bueno.* Now you may lower your hands and walk on up to the house. Inside we will have a little talk."

Jorge said in Spanish, "I do not understand. This is a stickup?" He used the English for the final phrase.

"No." Johnny's voice as yet held no real threat. "We just want to talk about why you were here the other time, what you were after, and who sent you."

"I?" Jorge said. "I have never been here before."

"That is a lie." Johnny's voice now held an edge. "Your footprints led to the house and away, over toward that tree where your car was parked. It was dark."

"My footprints?"

"Eso es. Plain as can be. The same footprints as now. And so we will talk. I will ask questions, and you will answer. Start walking." The rifle prodded gently at Jorge's back. "Walk," Johnny said again, this time with emphasis.

Jorge walked.

15

Mollie, watching, opened the door as they approached. She looked at Jorge, she looked at Johnny, and she looked at the rifle Johnny held. "I will make coffee," she said, and disappeared into the tiny kitchen.

Johnny closed the door. He gestured with the rifle. "Sit down." He took a chair facing Jorge's, the rifle resting comfortably across his knees. "Now we'll have some ID," he said. "A driver's license will do."

Slowly, reluctantly, his eyes never leaving the rifle, Jorge took out his wallet. He dropped his eyes momentarily to select his driver's license and hold it out. He watched Johnny glance at the picture, glance again at Jorge's face, then read the name. He held out the license, and Jorge took it back and replaced it in the wallet.

All the things he had heard about this cop, Jorge was thinking, had not quite prepared him for what he saw now. Part Indian, someone had told him, and that certainly was obvious in the aquiline nose, the high cheekbones, but, above all, in the dark eyes that glittered like polished stones as they studied Jorge's face, making him intensely uncomfortable.

"So," Johnny said at last. "Jorge Trujillo. *Bueno.* We will have much to talk about."

Jorge took a deep breath. "If I am under arrest," he said, "I have a right—" Something in Johnny's face stopped the words, and Jorge became silent.

"We will talk," Johnny said again. "I will ask questions. And you will answer them. You went to El Rancho motel. You talked with a man named Artie Gilmore, no?"

Jorge took another deep breath. "If I am charged—" he began, and again he stopped. Here in this little house with this man, the words would only sound empty. Besides, the words simply would not come out. Jorge sat mute.

"Yes?" Johnny said. "Or no?"

After a long pause, "Yes." Jorge's voice was almost a whisper.

"You told him that he was to leave town?"

"Yes."

"He did," Johnny said. "He went back to Miami. They found him floating in the water the other morning, face down."

Jorge opened his mouth and closed it again carefully. He licked his dry lips. "I had nothing to do with it," he said. "Believe me."

"Oh, I believe you. You were just the messenger, but I thought you would like to know what result your message produced."

Jorge swallowed and sat silent again.

"You take care of Bascomb's car," Johnny said.

"Yes."

"You service it?"

"Yes."

170

"Is it armor-plated?"

Jorge swallowed hard.

"Yes?" Johnny said. "Or no?"

"Yes."

"How do you know?"

"I . . . weighed . . . it. On the truck scales." The words came out with slow reluctance.

"Go on."

"It weighs 6,000 pounds. It has a special engine and—"

"That's enough. I don't want a course in automotive engineering."

The kitchen door opened and Mollie appeared carrying two cups of coffee. She placed one beside each man. "I have things to do," she said in her shy voice. "If there is anything you want?"

"Thanks," Johnny said. "We're getting along just fine." He waited until the door to the rear of the house closed. "Now the chopper," he said. "You fly it, yes?"

Jorge nodded.

"I am not going to ask you about a flight over Elk Ridge a little time back," Johnny said, "a night flight during which a dead man was dropped on the talus slope." He paused. "What I am going to ask you is, why does Bascomb have a chopper and you to fly it?"

"It's easier, faster than using the car." Jorge's voice was gaining confidence.

"To go where?"

Jorge managed a shrug. "Albuquerque, Las Cruces, like that."

"Any other places?"

Jorge nodded. "Sometimes Texas, Mexico. *El jefe* likes the seacoast."

"Arizona? California?"

"Sometimes."

"On these flights," Johnny said, "do you carry anything?"

Jorge's face looked blank, and then his expression took on a look of apprehension. "You mean drugs? Like that?"

"You catch on quick," Johnny said.

Jorge was shaking his head emphatically. "Never," he said. "I load the chopper. I know what we carry. It is only clothing, things for us both." His voice altered significantly, took on a pleading note. "Believe me."

"Oh," Johnny said, "I do. Bascomb wouldn't get his hands dirty. That's clear." His voice could have been carrying on a friendly conversation, but his eyes did not leave Jorge's face. "These are business trips?"

"Sí. I mean, yes."

"Spanish is all right. Business? All of them?"

Jorge shook his head. "Like I said, *el jefe* likes the seacoast. He swims. He snorkels. He goes fishing at Guaymas, like that."

Johnny nodded understandingly. "Now," he said, "we come to the other night when you broke in here." He raised one hand in a peremptory gesture. "No lies. Your footprints are plain as day. That was why I asked Mrs. Higgins to lead you here, where you would walk in the dirt and I could see your footprints. I would have recognized them anywhere. You may believe that."

Jorge sat silent, feeling numb. This, too, he had heard about this cop, that he could follow men into the mountains or the mesas merely by their tracks in the dirt as surely as a bloodhound is said to follow a man's scent.

"You were after something," Johnny said. "It was a wristwatch, no?"

Jorge swallowed hard. He said nothing.

"Yes?" Johnny said in that implacable voice. "Or no?"

Jorge nodded faintly and his lips formed the word, "Yes," but no sound came out. This man was a devil who knew all things. How, Jorge could not even guess.

"You stripped the body of the man who was dropped on Elk Ridge," Johnny said, "of everything, wallet, ID, weapon from his holster, keys, money, even his handkerchief—but you overlooked his wrist-watch." He shook his head gently. "No, you don't need to answer. I am not accusing you of anything—now. I am just stating facts." He paused again. "There were numbers engraved on the back of that wrist-watch. Did you know that?"

"No!" Jorge swallowed hard, realizing that he had been tricked into tacitly admitting that he knew of the watch. "I mean—"

"Never mind what you mean," Johnny said. "I believe you. But it was only because of the numbers that the watch was important. You may believe that, too. And you failed to find it here the other night. Don't even bother to answer that, either. I know it." He picked up his coffee cup and sipped from it thoughtfully. He set it down again. "Is there anything you would like to tell me, Jorge?"

Jorge opened his mouth and shut it again carefully. Once again he licked his dry lips. "Like what?"

"Why," Johnny said, "I don't know. Maybe when you think about Artie Gilmore and what happened to him, something might occur to you that you think I'd like to know." He nodded. *"Es possible?"*

Jorge hesitated. "I—" he began, and stopped. He shook his head emphatically. "No. *Nada*, nothing. I know nothing. I have nothing to tell."

Johnny nodded approvingly. "A man with a clean

conscience. I admire that." He was silent for long moments, watching Jorge's face steadily. He said at last, "Are you going to tell Bascomb about this little talk?"

Jorge closed his eyes. He opened them again and sat motionless, clearly uncertain, while those eyes of polished stone seemed to look right into his mind and through. He took a deep breath, the deepest. "No," he said.

Johnny nodded. "I agree. He might be upset." He gestured vaguely. "You may go, Jorge."

"Where?"

"Why, anywhere you like." Johnny smiled. It was not a pretty smile. "If we want you," he said, "we will find you. Wherever you are." He stood up. "That's all. *Hasta luego.*"

He watched Jorge get out of his chair, still clearly uncertain. His eyes went to the rifle in Johnny's hands.

"No," Johnny said, "I have no intention of shooting you and saying you were trying to escape. Open the door, walk out, and close it again. Nobody will bother you." He added, "This isn't Cuba. Or even Miami. *Adiós.*"

He watched the door open and close, and he watched Jorge walk slowly, uncertainly down the drive to the street. He heard the door behind him open and he said, "Come in, Mrs. Higgins. Our visitor has gone."

Mollie walked in. She wore her apologetic smile. "I—ah—listened," she said.

"I hoped you might. Did you learn anything?"

Mollie sat down. She folded her hands primly in her lap. "I learned," she said, "or, rather, I corroborated what I had already been quite sure of, and that is that

Mr. Bascomb is not a nice man—indeed, he is a very wicked man."

"That is exactly right," Johnny said.

"Can you prove it, Lieutenant?"

"Johnny, please. And the answer is, no, not yet, maybe not ever, although I hope I am wrong."

Mollie looked thoughtful. "In mathematics," she said, "it is very difficult to prove a negative. Do you understand what I am saying, Lieutenant—Johnny?"

"Quite well. It's hard in life, too. That's why we start with a presumption of innocence, and have to prove guilt."

"I hadn't thought of it that way," Mollie said slowly, "but, yes, I do see what you mean." She paused. "Maybe I can help. Somehow."

"I hope so," Johnny said. "I can use all the help I can get." He smiled gently. "Thank you for your help today. Call me, please, if you have any further—problems."

Mollie watched him walk down the drive, the rifle held loosely, easily in one hand. A strange man, she thought, unlike anyone she had ever known. It was comforting to know that he was, in a sense, on her side. As were others, and their support was equally comforting.

Lucille and Waldo Harrington, for example. They, too, were remarkable people, far more worldly than she was, more knowledgeable. She hesitated for only a few moments before she went to the telephone, looking at her watch as she did. Yes, it was time that the Harringtons were home from the Lab. She dialed their number quickly before she changed her mind.

Lucille answered in her calm voice. "This is Mollie Higgins," Mollie said.

"Yes, Mollie?" In the two words there was welcome, warm and comforting.

"I have something," Mollie said, "that I think I would like to tell you. And ask your advice." Her voice turned shy and diffident. "If that would not be too great an imposition?"

"Not at all," Lucille said. "Come right along, my dear. Waldo and I will be delighted to see you."

"Thank you," Mollie said. "Oh, thank you very much!"

Lucille answered the door with a smile and a comforting handshake. "Come in. Waldo and I are sitting on the *portal* admiring the view. Come join us."

Music, a Mozart quartet, played softly on the record player in the living room. From the *portal* the view was endless, and there was a faint, pleasant breeze stirring.

"Waldo and I are partial to martinis," Lucille said. "What would you like to drink, my dear?"

In her shy voice, "A martini would be fine." The apologetic smile appeared. "I like them on the rocks, with a twist of lemon. If that is not too much trouble?"

"Our tipple exactly," Waldo said, and headed for the wet bar.

"Sit down, dear," Lucille said.

Mollie sat down. "Your view is lovely." She felt ill at ease, and the words sounded somehow inane.

Lucille was smiling. "Relax," she said, "and as soon as Waldo comes back, tell us of your adventures. Oh, yes, Cassie has partially filled us in."

After that, it was easier. Martini at her elbow, sipping occasionally, Mollie recounted her trip to

Miami, the Bahamas, and Grand Cayman. "I found the bank account." She told about that, as she had told Cassie and Johnny in the car. When she mentioned the amount, both Lucille and Waldo smiled in surprise.

"You did hit the jackpot, didn't you?" Waldo said.

"All from the numbers on the back of the watch?" Lucille said. She nodded approvingly. "Well done."

"It was the combinations of the two-digit numbers," Mollie said. "Individually, there were simply too many possible combinations of the numbers to make sense."

Lucille nodded again. "Good thinking." She paused thoughtfully. "And the numbers of the account were also one of the combinations?"

"Yes. With an additional code word." Mollie hesitated. "But that is not all." She smiled apologetically. "Mr. Russell at the bank made an offer I, ah, couldn't refuse."

Lucille said gently, "And that was?"

"He said if there was anything he could do for me, anything at all." Mollie colored visibly. "I mean, it was the size of the account on deposit, not anything about me, that prompted his offer."

"Understood," Lucille said. "That much money does impress a banker."

"So," Mollie said, "I—ah—took him up on it." She told them what she had asked Mr. Russell to do.

Lucille leaned back in her chair, smiling. "I am very proud of you, Mollie dear," she said. "You are going to be a great addition to the Lab. Ingenuity like that is hard to find."

"Damn near nonexistent," Waldo said. "I bow to your quick wit."

"Now," Lucille said, "let us put our heads together and see how this advantage can best be exploited. I believe that is the way to proceed?"

"Hear, hear," Waldo said.

"Oh," Mollie said, "thank you, thank you very much. I hoped you would see it that way!"

Tony Lopez walked into Johnny's office and leaned against the wall. He was smiling cheerfully. "On that matter you asked me to attend to," he said, "the records you wish?"

"Go on," Johnny said.

"I have located a *prima*," Tony said. "We are not closely related, and I do not know her well. Yet."

"And?"

"And she turns out to be *muy guapa*, in fact, *guapíssima*." The word *guapa* connotes sexiness along with beauty. "I was not aware that my family had produced such a *chica*."

Johnny could smile. "You will impress her, I'm sure."

"I intend to try, *amigo*. The records you seek will cost me an expensive dinner or two, I am sure." Tony spread his hands and showed white teeth in a broad grin. "But under the circumstances, I will make the sacrifice willingly."

"*Buen suerte,* good luck," Johnny said.

16

They finished a second martini. "You will stay for dinner," Lucille told Mollie, and smiled. "Leftovers, I'm afraid."

"Lu," Waldo said, "does incredible things with leftovers. And one of our extravagances is our wine cellar, so perhaps that is an added inducement."

"You are too kind," Mollie said. "Thank you very much. I would love to stay."

"And," Lucille said, "I think we are agreed on the plan of action?"

"I believe it fits the bill very neatly," Waldo said. He wore a pensive look. "I am afraid I had not realized before what an unpleasant person this Leon Bascomb seems to be." He paused reflectively, and both women watched him. "He could very well be dangerous," Waldo said at last. "Personally dangerous, I mean. And you, Mollie, will be the person in jeopardy if he is."

Mollie produced her apologetic smile. "Someone has to do it."

Lucille said, "I am afraid that is entirely too true."

"Will Johnny cooperate?" Waldo said. "I am not

179

having second thoughts, but I am trying to consider all possibilities."

"If Mollie asks him," Lucille said, "Johnny will cooperate. I am confident of that."

"I will ask him," Mollie said.

Lucille stood up. "I believe it is settled then." She smiled. "I will see about stirring up some dinner. You two sit here and enjoy the view." She made a gesture of denial. "No, Mollie, no help, thanks. I like to work alone in the kitchen." She was gone.

Waldo said to Mollie, "Obviously you feel very strongly about Bascomb." It was a statement, no question, but it asked for an answer.

"I am afraid I do," Mollie said. "I feel as if Walter and I have been treated as if we were nonpersons, as they say, or used to say in Communist countries, and I resent that. I am not a nonperson, and neither was Walter." There was firmness in her voice. "Mr. Bascomb is obviously used to taking what he wants and, yes, destroying those who stand in his way. I will not countenance that." The apologetic smile appeared, and her voice turned diffident. "If you see what I mean?"

"I enjoy reading history," Waldo said. "And there have been times without number when some single person has decided that he has had enough of tyranny, oppression, and has risen against it. Not infrequently, others have followed his lead and the entire course of history has been altered." He smiled. "Who knows what may come from your, ah—determination? Which, I might add, I find admirable, wholly admirable."

"Thank you very much," Mollie said. "I am flattered."

* * *

180

Jorge had changed his mind. It would be better, he decided, if he did tell Bascomb of his session with Johnny in the Higgins house, after all. The cop had been right when he had said that he, Jorge, might do well to think about what had happened to Artie Gilmore. Jorge did not like the idea of being found floating face down in some lake or stream.

Bascomb, behind his desk in his book-lined study, listened quietly without visible reaction. When Jorge was finished, "I am glad you told me," Bascomb said. "You are sure you told him nothing?"

"The trips," Jorge said, "when I fly you to Albuquerque, Las Cruces, Guaymas, and like that. That is all."

"He didn't ask you about the body on Elk Ridge?"

"No." The cop had not asked him, Jorge thought, he had *told* him; there was a difference.

"All right," Bascomb said. "That is all."

Bascomb waited until the door was closed again before he allowed himself to give vent to what he felt. That goddamned cop and that goddamned innocuous-looking little Mollie Higgins! Everywhere he, Bascomb, looked, the two of them seemed to be there staring at him as if he were something impaled on the point of a pin. They were—nothing! A hicktown cop and a computer programmer, people he could buy and sell without even feeling the cash pinch.

They were no real threat. He had thought carefully and decided that. But they were an annoyance, and there were limits to his patience. Artie Gilmore had flubbed the job. Maybe, little as he liked the idea, it was time that he took matters into his own hands. It had been proved time and time again: If you wanted something done right, you had damn well better do it yourself.

Tony walked into Johnny's office bearing a stack of computer printout pages. "Do I look like the cat that has stolen the cream, *amigo?*" he said.

Johnny nodded. "A reasonable facsimile. What have you there?"

"The records you wished." Tony laid the stack gently on Johnny's desk. "Ask me no questions, and I will tell you no lies. I will say only that the dinner *was* expensive, but it was well worth it."

"If you mean what I think you mean," Johnny said, "I'll just say that messing around with your own cousin isn't considered quite the thing to do."

Tony's cheerful grin remained intact. "I told you that we are only distantly related." He gestured at the stack of papers. "That *is* what you wished, no?"

Johnny was already scanning the pages, reading swiftly. *"Madre de Dios!"* he said.

Tony crossed himself.

"No blasphemy intended," Johnny said. "Just an expression of surprise." He bent over the pages again, turning them down swiftly, scanning the neat columns of names, places, dates. Without looking up, "Call Howard, the DEA man in Albuquerque," he said. "Tell him I'm on my way down." He pushed back his chair and stood up. "And no word of this to anybody. *Entendido?*"

"Claro," Tony said. "Is important, yes?"

"Very," Johnny said. "It is, I think, what we have been looking for for a long time."

All during the sixty-mile drive, the stack of printout pages on the seat beside him, Johnny tried to hold his excitement in check while he went over and over again the entire list of possibilities the pages opened up. Right under my nose, he told himself, right under all our noses. Or was this just another wrong guess? He thought not, but only time and careful examination would tell.

Howard, the DEA man, looked at the printout pages slowly, methodically, making no notes, but from time to time turning back to check something he had already read, and then going on. When he was finished, he leaned back in his chair and looked at Johnny. "I don't suppose you want to tell me how you got this?"

"No. And I don't think you want to ask. Let's just say it came into my hands."

Howard nodded. "It will have to be checked, of course."

Johnny nodded. "And it could turn out to mean nothing."

"It could," Howard said, and added without reservation, "but I sure as hell doubt it. All those part-load shipments from those little seacoast towns, and then transshipped to towns nobody ever heard of in western Arizona, California; innocent household goods, folks moving west—" He shook his head. "There aren't that many people either in the towns of origin or in the towns of destination, but who looks twice at a moving van?"

Johnny said, "There are check stations along the way."

"They check weight, nothing else. And even if some snoopy guy looked inside, what would he see? Chairs, tables, beds, boxes of household stuff, collapsible wardrobes filled with clothes." He paused. "With maybe, no, probably, kilos of coke stashed in each part-load, a little here, a little there." He shook his head.

"Dogs," Johnny said. "I've heard about them."

"Sure. We've got them, trained to sniff out dope. But who'd think to use them in a moving van?" Howard shook his head again. "Neat, simple, obvious —except it took you to sniff it out."

"We aren't there yet," Johnny said.

"No. But this is a better direction than we've had in some time." Howard was silent, thoughtful. "You think Bascomb set this up? Runs it? From Santo Cristo? That was what you meant by talking about that canyon that became a center a thousand years ago?" He nodded. "I see it now, the connection."

Johnny said, "Maybe we can tie Bascomb in, and maybe we can't."

"You sound disappointed."

"I am. He's the one I want."

Howard glanced again at the pages. "Todd Van and Storage," he said.

"Joe Todd was almost broke," Johnny said. "I found that out. Never mind how." Bert Clancy. "Then Bascomb came along with a big, fat loan, and connections in Texas, Louisiana, other places. Todd's business began to pick up."

"You think Todd's innocent, doesn't even know what he's doing?"

"It figures." Johnny shook his head faintly. "But the way I see it, even if it blows up, Todd's the fall guy, no? It's Bascomb's money and connections, yes, but who's to prove he knew, really knew, what was going on?"

Howard smiled without amusement. "You sound more than disappointed. You sound bitter."

"I am. Bascomb killed Higgins, the FBI man. I

know it. He's responsible for killing another man—or maybe I am, at least partly, but Bascomb was behind it. He's scum, worse than scum, but I'm not sure we can even lay a hand on him."

Howard stood up. "Let's make a call on Gus Goddard." He picked up the printout pages. "With these. We'll talk about federal warrants, and with them we can throw a wide net, real wide. Maybe your friend Bascomb will be caught in it."

"I wouldn't bet on it," Johnny said.

Tony Lopez was summoned to take the phone call. It was Mrs. Mollie Higgins. "The lieutenant's down in Albuquerque, Mrs. Higgins," he said. "He called and said he'd be a few days. Can it wait?"

"I suppose it will have to," Mollie Higgins said. "I'm sure what the lieutenant is doing is very important, and I wouldn't want to disturb him."

"No, ma'am."

"But when he does return—" It was the shy, diffident voice. "—will you please ask him if he could call me? If it isn't too much trouble, that is."

"No trouble at all," Tony said. "I'm sure he'll call as soon as he can."

"Thank you. Thank you very much indeed, Sergeant Lopez. You are very kind."

Tony hung up and looked at the desk sergeant. "Every so often, one like her comes along," he said, "and ruins my bad opinion of most Anglos."

Federal Magistrate Gus Goddard finished reading the printout sheets, leaned back in his chair, and looked at Howard and Johnny. "Hardly conclusive," he said, "but definitely suggestive."

Howard said, "We know that far more drugs get

through than we intercept. What we haven't known is how."

"And this," the judge said, "you think may be an explanation?"

"One of them, at least," Howard said. "I'd bet on it."

"And what are you suggesting?"

"That we throw a net around those suspect places of origin," Howard said, "and another around those suspect destinations, and see what we come up with."

"And Santo Cristo? This Todd Van and Storage?"

"If dope originates at Point A and arrives at Point C, we can show that it went through Point B on the way, where it was off-loaded and then loaded again. That's enough for now. Besides, we don't want to get Bascomb's wind up prematurely. He could just disappear, and maybe turn up somewhere else beyond our reach."

The judge looked at Johnny. "You concur, Lieutenant?"

"This is all out of my line," Johnny said. "But, yes, it makes sense, as far as it goes."

"That sounds like reluctant acquiescence," the judge said.

Johnny nodded. "In a way, it is. I want Bascomb on a murder charge, and while this is all very well and I'm completely in favor of it, it doesn't get me any closer to Bascomb."

The judge smiled. "You're a hunter, Lieutenant."

"Yes, sir. When I pick up a trail, I like to follow it. To the end."

"And in the meantime?"

"Why," Johnny said, "I'll help with this all I can. I

have sources close to Todd—" Tony Lopez and his *prima.* "—and I can maybe supply information that could be useful."

The judge looked at Howard. Howard said, "Offer gratefully accepted. Local authorities can be a nuisance—" He smiled. "—just as sometimes we're a damn nuisance to them. But this is a special case, and we'll do best working together."

The judge thought about it. Presently he nodded. "Tell me what you need," he said.

Cassie said, "I'm worried." She and Mollie were again having lunch together.

"About your Johnny?"

Cassie smiled and shook her head. "He can take care of himself. I'm worried about you. Sooner or later Leon will find out that you know about his offshore bank account."

"Inevitably," Mollie said, and smiled in apology for her certainty.

"And he wouldn't want you talking about it. It's supposed to be secret."

"True." Mollie was smiling no longer.

"And then," Cassie said, "oh, I know it sounds farfetched, but you and Johnny have me convinced that Leon himself is farfetched, so he just might—"

"Kill me as he killed Walter?" Mollie's tone was firm.

"Exactly."

Again the apologetic smile. "I had thought of it," Mollie said. She hesitated. "Are you suggesting that I go into hiding?"

Cassie was smiling again. "No," she said. "Something far better than that. When we finish lunch, you go home and pack a few things in a bag." The smile spread. "Think of it as a weekend in the country. Someone will pick you up."

Mollie was frowning.

"Don't argue," Cassie said. "I hate to use the phrase, but, trust me."

Ben Hart's great dusty Cadillac swept into Mollie's drive, and Ben himself got out to walk to the door. When it opened, he looked down, almost filling the doorway, smiling. "You're a little one, aren't you?" he said. He held out a big hand. "I'm Ben Hart, and Cassie told me I'd like you. That's good enough for me. This your bag? Come along. Nobody's going to bother you, little lady, and they better not even try."

In the car, "Just a few days," Ben said. "Until Johnny gets back and decides what we do next. You ride?"

The big old man seemed unreal, Mollie thought, but there was also something comforting about him and his breezy certainty. "Horseback?" she said. "I have. Not well, of course."

"Got me a mare," Ben said. "Cassie rides her sometimes. Nice and friendly. Gentle, too. You'll like her, and she'll like you. Horses know people almost better than we know them. You'll get along."

Jorge said, "She was seen driving out to his ranch with Señor Hart. That was yesterday. She has not come back."

"She's staying out there?" Bascomb said. "Good. Then I know where to find her." He studied Jorge's face. "You are thinking what?"

Jorge said slowly, "Señor Hart is best not molested. It is well known."

"Nonsense," Bascomb said. "That is all."

He drove the heavy Cadillac with care along the graded road in from Ben Hart's cattle guard, and realized that he had had no idea of the amount of space Ben's ranch occupied. The land was rolling and seemingly without end. Here and there a windmill turned lazily in the faint breeze, assuring the nearby stock tank of ample water. Cattle in groups of three or four dotted the landscape. Behind him, in the mirror, he could see the great, brooding mountains that lay behind Santo Cristo. Out here he felt naked and exposed, even in his steel and tinted-glass cocoon.

When he came over the final rise and saw the ranch house, he stopped involuntarily, impressed by the size of the building with its stone walls and expanses of glass, the corrals and outbuildings that surrounded it, the air of easy efficiency that seemed to permeate the sight.

There was a huge, graveled parking area and a single car within it. Bascomb parked the Cadillac, got out, and walked up to the house. Ben Hart himself, huge and relaxed, answered the thud of the ponderous iron door knocker. "Well, well," Ben said. "Looky who's here." His voice was neither friendly nor unfriendly.

Behind Ben another voice said, "Well, ask the man in. Let's see what he has in mind." Congressman Hawley's voice.

"Why, sure," Ben said. "Come on in and have a look-see." He held the door wide.

It was, Bascomb decided, the largest living room he

had ever seen, two-storied, galleried, beamed, with trophies mounted over the huge fireplace—mountain goat, bighorn sheep, an elk head with a wider spread of antlers than Bascomb had ever imagined, and, next to it, the snarling head of what had to be a grizzly bear broad enough for two large hands to be placed between the ears.

"I mostly gave up hunting some time ago," Ben Hart said. "Sort of lost the taste for it. But I keep these around anyway, kind of like old friends."

Bascomb also noted the gun case against the wall with its row of rifles and shotguns and, hanging from pegs, handguns in their worn holsters. The place seemed like, and was, a fortress, and all at once the two old men appeared in a different light, totally at home in these surroundings, no doubt as familiar with the guns in the case as they were with the decanter of whisky on the table between two chairs.

"A mite different from that palace of yours," Mark Hawley said, "but, then, you're a civilized man. We're just a couple of country boys, and Ben here likes room to move around in."

Ben said, "You're looking at the bear?" He waited for no answer. "Johnny was with me when I got him. Johnny Ortiz, the police feller. I'm not too bad a tracker myself, but I'm nowhere near his class. We followed that bear two days and a night, and Johnny never lost the trail. I'd purely hate to have him tracking me."

The congressman said, "Aren't you going to offer the man some drinking whisky? Where're your manners?"

"No, thanks," Bascomb said. "I don't take hard liquor."

"I could probably scare up some wine," Ben said. "We got a few cases stashed around."

Bascomb shook his head and smiled. "I just came—" He paused. "—out of curiosity. I had heard about your ranch, of course. I must say I am impressed."

"Nothing special in mind?" Ben said.

"No. I was just out for a drive, passing by."

"You like to look around," Ben said, "I'll have one of the boys show you the corrals and the barns and such."

Mark Hawley said, "Maybe the man'd just like to set a spell and talk. Ben and I weren't powwowing about anything special. I get back from Washington, I like to hear about what's happened here on my home ground."

Bascomb said, "I won't interrupt any more. I am grateful for the look."

"Suit yourself," Ben said. "We ate your food and drank your liquor, and turnabout's fair play. Come again, if you like. If I'm not here, there's always some of the ranch hands."

Was there a warning there? Bascomb wondered. He decided that there definitely was, as there had been in the mention of that damned cop and his tracking ability. "Thank you," he said. "Western hospitality." He walked back out into the sun, and the heavy door closed behind him with a solid sound.

Mark Hawley said, "How do you figure it?"

"Wanted to see the lay of the land," Ben said, and there was a low growl beneath the words.

"Think he'll come back?"

"I kind of hope he does. And not just to look."

"You could mount his head up with the others."

"No," Ben said. "I'd rather nail his hide to the barn door." He jerked his head toward the fireplace. "Those were decent animals. I wouldn't insult them with his company."

Mollie appeared behind the upstairs gallery railing. "Come on down, little lady," Ben said. "Our visitor's gone."

17

Johnny said, "Here are two part-loads in transit from Todd in Santo Cristo to the Barstow area in California. Both part-loads originated in our Texas Gulf town. Look interesting?"

"I would say definitely," Howard said. "They're due to arrive when?"

"Late today. Or tomorrow at the latest. I'd have given more warning, but we're trying not to tip our hand."

Howard smiled. "Understood. And this is plenty of time. We'll check it out tonight." His smile spread. "I'm afraid I can't tell you exactly how."

"I wouldn't want to know," Johnny said. "You hunt your way. I'll hunt mine." He paused thoughtfully. "But if it checks out, mind telling me what comes next?"

"We move in on Texas. Ditto Louisiana. There has to be a stash somewhere, a big one, and we'll find it. Meanwhile we'll lower the boom in California on those who've been receiving the loads. We have a number already targeted. There's one trucking firm that has its own depot in L.A. It looks promising."

"You've been busy," Johnny said.

"So have you. And I guess I don't have to say how much we appreciate it."

"Let's see if it pans out first."

"It will," Howard said. His voice was confident. "I've got a strong hunch about this. You ever get hunches?"

Johnny thought of Tony Lopez and found it hard not to smile. "Sometimes." He made a gesture of finality. "I think I've done what I can here. I'll head back up the hill to my own turf." He paused. "You'll let me know how it comes out?"

"Done and done. And if there's any way we can help you tie Bascomb in, just shout."

Johnny drove the pickup homeward without haste. It was funny how things worked out sometimes, how they began and how they developed. It had been Cassie's mind jumping to Chaco Canyon and, when seen from the air, the roads like wheel spokes leading to it, roads traveled a thousand years ago, no one knew exactly why, that had begun his own thinking about what could possibly make Santo Cristo a center that would attract Bascomb. Tenuous beginning, and the evidence getting stronger as they followed the trail. He felt as confident as Howard did that they were right on course.

But that still left Bascomb with his armor-plated Cadillac and his big house and his seemingly impregnable reputation as a businessman. Those in Louisiana and Texas who originated the part-loads might suffer, as would those who received the shipments, and Joe Todd, who had handled the transshipments. But Bascomb? Johnny's face was suddenly set in its harsh Indian lines. Bascomb's hands probably wouldn't even be soiled. There was the bitter fact.

He topped the La Bajada rise and plucked the microphone from its hook to call headquarters and ask for Tony. "I'm coming in," he said. "With you and your *prima* helping, we may have wrapped it up." He could smile ruefully. "I'll buy the dinner this time, you, your *prima,* and Cassie."

"Bueno." There was happy satisfaction in Tony's voice. It changed and became businesslike. "The little Mrs. Higgins is anxious to talk to you," Tony said.

Johnny nodded. "I'll stop and see her. She is home?"

"No. She is out at Ben Hart's ranch. For protection."

Bascomb again, Johnny thought, and the harsh Indian lines reappeared in his face. "I'll stop there, then. Over and out."

He drove the pickup rattling in over Ben's cattle guard and raised a dust plume the eight miles to the ranch house. He wondered what Mollie Higgins wanted, and decided that with the little woman there was no telling.

Resourceful was one of the words that came to mind when you thought of her, witness that fainting episode in La Guardia Airport. *Indomitable* was another word, and that brought to memory her pursuit of the bank account in Miami, the Bahamas, and Grand Cayman. Mollie Higgins was a very complex little package, and there was simply no telling which way she would turn next.

Ben answered Johnny's knock. "Welcome, stranger," he said, and held the door wide.

Mollie was there, smiling her shy smile, and seeming, in these large surroundings, even smaller than usual.

"I got your message," Johnny said.

"I hope I didn't inconvenience you."

"Not a bit."

"Got time to set a spell?" Ben Hart said. "Nothing's been happening, except maybe the little lady's a mite sore from riding."

"I'm fine," Mollie said. "It was like being in a rocking chair." She hesitated, and the shyness appeared. "Would it be all right," she said, "if I went back into town with the lieutenant? You've been most kind, and I do appreciate it."

"But you got things to attend to," Ben said. "Understood. You run right along, but be sure you come back, hear? You've brightened the place up."

In the pickup, "He is such a dear," Mollie said. "A big, lovable bear, that's what he is."

"Most times," Johnny said, "yes. Other times . . ." He smiled. "Let's just say he's a good man to have on your side, not against you."

Mollie was thoughtful. "Mr. Bascomb came out," she said.

"Did he now?" Johnny's voice was sharp with interest.

"Nothing happened. He and Ben and Mark Hawley just talked."

Johnny glanced at the woman's face. There was something beneath her words. "But what?"

"I listened," Mollie said. "And, well, I can't describe it, but there was—tension. It was palpable."

"But nothing happened? Then Ben was on his good behavior. And Mark. Otherwise Bascomb would have had his head handed to him on a platter." He paused, thinking about it, and wishing it *had* been that way. "Anyway," he said, "I'll bet Bascomb got whatever point they were trying to make."

Mollie said, "And you are wondering why I wanted

to see you." The shyness was again plain. "I have a favor to ask." She hesitated. "I would very much like to have you hear a telephone call I want to make."

Johnny was silent, waiting.

"To Mr. Bascomb," Mollie said, as if that explained all. "Will it be too much trouble for you?"

"I think I can stand it," Johnny said, and wondered what it was that rang a bell so clearly in his mind. Well, there was only one way to find out. "Your house?"

"If you please," Mollie said in her small, diffident voice.

The little house seemed stuffy after being shut up for a few days. "I'll open some windows," Johnny said, and did. When he had finished, he looked at Mollie, who was seated at the telephone, smiling hesitantly.

"I am ready," she said, "if you are." She picked up the phone and dialed quickly, the number obviously already well in mind. Her voice was firm when she said, "This is Mrs. Walter Higgins. I should like to speak to Mr. Bascomb, please."

That bell was still ringing insistently, Johnny thought as he watched and listened, but even now he had no idea what the woman was up to.

"Hello," Mollie said. "Mr. Bascomb?" Her voice was diffident now. "Perhaps you remember me? We met at a gallery opening." She held the phone a little distance from her ear, and Johnny could hear Bascomb's voice clearly.

"I remember," Bascomb said. His tone was wary.

"I was away for a little time," Mollie said. "I was in Miami."

"So?"

"And the Bahamas."

Bascomb's voice took on more than a hint of impatience. "What is the purpose of this call?"

"And Grand Cayman," Mollie said. "It is a charming place. There are many banks."

"Get to the point!"

"One bank in particular," Mollie said. "There was a very nice gentleman named Mr. Russell. Do you know him, Mr. Bascomb?"

"No. And what does all this have to do with me?"

"There is a numbered bank account there," Mollie said. "And aside from the number, there is a code word that must be produced."

"I repeat, what does all this have to do with me?"

"The precise balance in the account," Mollie said, "was $21,598,432.14. Of course, that will undoubtedly have changed by now. A sum that large accumulates interest quite quickly."

There was a pause. Bascomb said at last, "I haven't the faintest idea what you are talking about."

"Oh, dear," Mollie said. "You haven't? Then probably you are not interested in knowing that I had the account number changed. And the code word. Mr. Russell was very obliging. The old number and code word would be expunged from their records, he said—that was his word, expunged—and the new number and code word programmed into their computer." She paused. "But if you don't know anything about it, why, of course you are not interested, and I am sorry to have bothered you, Mr. Bascomb. Please forgive me. Good-bye." She hung up and sat quiet, smiling shyly at Johnny.

"Madre de Dios!" Johnny said, and shook his head in slow wonder. "You actually did have the number changed?"

"Yes. And the code word."

"Then what you have done," Johnny said, "is throw a rock right into the bear's den and dare him to come out. You do see that, don't you?"

Mollie smiled apologetically. "I thought it might provoke a reaction."

"It will," Johnny said. "It will indeed. That's his backup money, the whole bundle, and—" He stopped and smiled. "You've thought it all the way through, haven't you? Are you turning it over to me?"

"We thought it was the best plan."

"We?"

"Lucille and Waldo Harrington and I."

"Bueno," Johnny said. His thoughts now were a high, fierce chant. At last, at last! "This is what I want you to do . . ."

It was dusk. Behind Santo Cristo the tops of the great mountains were still lighted by the last rays of sun, but in the city itself night was slowly settling in, and the vapor-filled dusk-to-dawn streetlights in the center of town were beginning to light up.

Johnny and Ben Hart sat in Johnny's pickup on a quiet dirt road well behind Mollie's house amid piñon and juniper trees and silence. "He'll wait for full darkness," Johnny said, his voice quiet, "but just to be sure, I've got Tony Lopez watching the house. He'll give us the word when Bascomb leaves."

"Was it me," Ben said, "I think I'd smell a rat."

"With twenty million dollars at stake?"

Ben thought about it. "That does change things a mite," he said. "How do these numbered bank accounts work?"

"No names," Johnny said. "I checked that with Bert Clancy. Just the right numbers and, in this case, a code word, too. Until Bascomb has the right numbers and the right code word, the money's beyond his reach." He smiled in the near-darkness. "That's what little Mollie Higgins has done to him."

"A stout little lady." Ben's voice held admiration. "She'd do to ride fence with." He was silent for a little time. He said at last, "You didn't say what you wanted me here for, boy, or what you want me to do."

"I wanted a witness, one who'd be believed."

"You think the man will talk?" Ben's voice was skeptical.

"You've met him," Johnny said. "What would you say his mainspring is?"

"Man's pretty full of himself."

"Exactly. And how do you think he'll react to being outsmarted by Mollie Higgins?"

Ben's soft chuckle came from deep in his chest. "About like a good horse the first time he feels a saddle on his back, and a rider—mean mad."

"Yes. He'll try his damnedest to show Mollie what a big, important fellow he is."

"And then what?" Ben's voice was quiet. "He'll just leave it like that and walk away?"

"No," Johnny said. "He'll have other plans." His voice, too, was serious. "And if they're violent—"

The police radio came alive and Tony Lopez's voice said, "He's leaving. At least, the car is."

Johnny raised the microphone. "Is he alone?"

"With those dark windows," Tony said, "there's no way to tell. The car could be full. You want me to follow him?"

"No. We can handle it. Over and out." Johnny hung up the microphone.

Ben said, "Taking quite a chance, aren't you, boy, setting the little lady up as coyote bait?"

He was, Johnny thought, and he knew it well. But

even if the DEA plans went through and turned out to be right, with drugs found in the two part-load shipments out in the California desert, there still would be no way to tie Bascomb in to the business. He would have covered his trail entirely too well. "There is no other way," he said, "to get the man to open himself up. Mollie will have to do it."

Ben said, "Got me a shooting iron in my car. Think maybe I'd best get it." He opened the door, slid out, and disappeared in the darkness. He was back shortly in complete silence, buckling a gun belt low around his hips. Johnny slid out of the truck, the 30-30 carbine in his hand. "Lead away," Ben said. His voice was a low growl.

Lights were on in Mollie's little house. From behind the house, through an open window and the open bedroom door, there was a clear view of the living room. Mollie was sitting with a book in her small hands. Johnny said, "I'll stay here."

Ben said, "Think maybe I'd best go around the side. Just in case." He was gone, silent for all his size. The night was still.

Distantly a car's engine sounded. It came closer and closer, and then stopped. There was the heavy sound of a door closing, the same sound, Johnny thought, he had noticed before, as Charlie Cottrell, the Cadillac dealer, had. And then a second door closed with the same solid *thunk*. So, Johnny thought, he had brought a backup. Ben would take care of that. Ben was, and had always been, a man to ride with.

Waiting crouched in the darkness, the rifle held at the ready in his hands, Johnny wondered what thoughts were going through little Mollie Higgins's mind as she no doubt heard the sounds of the car doors closing outside. There was simply no telling, he decided; the woman was an enigma, as full of surprises as a piñon nut was of meat.

Nor was there any way of knowing from her reactions whether fear or determination was uppermost in her feelings. As Cassie had said, Mollie could change with such bewildering speed from apologetic shyness to firmness that even trying to keep up with her moods was next to impossible.

When the knock came at the front door, Mollie put down her book with no show of emotion and went to answer it. Her shy voice reached Johnny clearly. "Why, Mr. Bascomb," she said. "This *is* a surprise."

"No, it is not," Bascomb said. "As you know perfectly well." There was anger in his voice, as Ben had predicted—a man mean mad. He closed the door behind him. He was alone. "I called the bank in Grand Cayman," he said. "You actually did have the account number changed, damn you."

"*And* the code word," Mollie said calmly. "As I told you on the phone, Mr. Bascomb. I saw no reason to lie."

Beside Johnny, Ben's voice whispered, "One man. He'll keep."

Johnny nodded without taking his eyes from the living room scene. He held the rifle loosely in both hands, tensed and ready for action.

"You represented yourself as my wife," Bascomb said, the anger now even plainer than before.

"I did not," Mollie said. "I told the young man that names were not important, but if he chose he could call me Mrs. Smith. That was all."

"I want the new number," Bascomb said. "And the code word."

"Somehow," Mollie said, and her voice now contained the hint of a smile, "I thought you would. That is a great deal of money, Mr. Bascomb. You must have gone to considerable trouble to accumulate it. How did you manage?"

"That is my business."

"But I believe Walter knew." The smile in her voice was gone. "My husband, Mr. Bascomb, in case you have forgotten."

"That son of a bitch!"

"You are maligning your own mother, Mr. Bascomb. Walter was your brother."

"He was," Bascomb said. "And my own brother was going to try to put me behind bars. My own brother!"

"And so you killed him." Mollie's voice was suddenly soft with anger. "The mark of Cain is very clear on your forehead, Mr. Bascomb. And fratricide is a mortal sin, is it not?"

The polished exterior of the man was beginning to disintegrate, Johnny thought, and what showed now was the naked viciousness. He raised the rifle slightly. "I killed him, yes," Bascomb said. "Without hesitation."

"As you intend to kill me?"

"You are beginning to get the idea."

"But," Mollie said, "only *after* I give you the new account number. And the new code word. I think the money is too important to you for it to be otherwise. But why should I tell you the number and code word, Mr. Bascomb? You are not a very nice man. In fact, I think you are a very wicked man indeed. Why should I help you?"

"You will," Bascomb said. "Believe me, you will. You are going to disappear."

"And be dropped from a helicopter as Walter was? That was unnecessary, Mr. Bascomb. It was a vicious thing to do."

Beside him, Johnny heard the faint click of the hammer of Ben's old-fashioned Frontier model .45 being cocked. He put a cautioning hand on Ben's arm.

"We are going to walk out of here," Bascomb said. A large gun had appeared from beneath his jacket. "Move!"

"No," Mollie said, "I don't believe we are. You see, I am not a thief, Mr. Bascomb, as you no doubt are. I never intended to take your money from the account, and now I intend to give it back to you by letting you have the new number and the new code word."

"Where are they?"

"Why, in my head, Mr. Bascomb. Numbers are my business. I remember them easily. Would you like me to write them down for you?"

"Don't play the tease with me, you *hija de puta!*"

Mollie's voice changed, hardened. "I know a little Spanish, Mr. Bascomb. You call me a daughter of a whore. But my mother was a very nice woman. She would have had nothing to do with you. Or your kind. She would have felt toward you just as Walter did, and I do—with contempt. Are you going to shoot me now, Mr. Bascomb? Before you learn the account number?"

Mollie turned then and crossed the room to a side table, opened the drawer, and took out a pad of paper and a pen. She wrote quickly, tore off the top page, and held it out. "Here, as I promised, are both the new number and the code word. You may have them. I am sure it is dirty money, and I want no part of it."

Bascomb stood motionless, frowning.

"Take it, Mr. Bascomb," Mollie said. "It is what you wanted, is it not? I am a person of my word, not a liar and a thief. Here." She held the paper out with a steady hand.

In Johnny's ear, Ben's voice whispered, "Boy, howdy, that is one stout little lady!"

Johnny nodded. Stout, he thought, *and* unpredictable, and what was running around the edges of his mind suddenly sounded a warning bell. He held the rifle at the ready and carefully watched Bascomb step forward, reach for and take the paper, look down to read it.

Mollie's hand moved swiftly. Oh, migod, Johnny thought, I should have seen it!

There was a sharp crack from the .25-caliber Banker's Special that had suddenly appeared in Mollie's hand. It was followed by two more shots.

Bascomb stiffened, and his mouth dropped open in surprise. His gun fell to the floor as he pressed both hands to his belly. Blood trickled from the corner of his mouth.

"You killed my husband, Mr. Bascomb," Mollie said, and her voice now was hard, unforgiving. "No doubt you have killed others as well. You have come here to threaten me. You are, as I said, a very wicked man indeed and you do not deserve to live. You will not." The little automatic cracked three more times.

"Jesus H Jumping Christ!" Ben's voice said in Johnny's ear.

"We go in," Johnny said, and went through the open window.

Ben disappeared around the side of the house.

Bascomb was still on his feet, but teetering and still clutching his belly. Blood oozed between his fingers.

As Johnny reached the open bedroom doorway, Bascomb went down, falling forward all at once, as a tree falls. His heels came up a little when he hit the floor, but that was the only movement he made.

Ben Hart appeared at the front door, pushing ahead of him, one large hand around the man's neck, Jorge Trujillo, whose eyes were not quite in focus. Jorge blinked twice when he saw Bascomb's body on the floor, then crossed himself, and his lips began to move in a prayer.

Mollie's expression was unfathomable as she held out the little automatic, and her voice told nothing. "You will want this, will you not, Lieutenant?" she said.

Johnny hesitated. He glanced down at the body on the floor, looked again at Mollie, and slowly shook his head. "No," he said, "a clear case of self-defense." With his toe he nudged the gun Bascomb had dropped. "Uzi submachine gun," he said. "Illegal and, worse, *sin duda,* without doubt, the weapon that killed your husband. Ballistic tests will show."

He walked then to the chair where Mollie had been sitting and picked up the book that had been in her hands, opened it, and took two reels of tape from the tape recorder that had been inside. "We won't need this, either," he said.

Mollie still watched him quietly with that unfathomable expression. The woman was unbelievable, Johnny thought, a combination of fearful desert pocket mouse and wildcat, totally unpredictable, totally beyond comprehension. He shook his head in slow wonder. "You," he said, "are something else."

"He was not a nice man." Mollie's voice now was apologetic.

"No," Johnny said, "he was not." He paused. "I think that is as good an epitaph as any."

18

It was morning, a Saturday. Johnny, Cassie, Mollie, Ben Hart, and Waldo and Lucille Harrington sat in the Harringtons' living room.

"Wouldn't have missed this powwow for the world," Ben Hart said. "I want the i's dotted and the t's crossed. Never did like puzzles that wouldn't come out."

Lucille said in her quiet, confident voice, "I daresay we will hear it all. Johnny, I believe, knows all the facts." She looked around the room. "Coffee, anyone?"

There was silence. Johnny looked around at them all. "I am not too proud of this whole business," he said. "I overlooked things I should have seen."

"Like what, boy?" This was Ben Hart. "Seems like it all came out pretty good."

Johnny made a gesture that dismissed Ben's words. "First," he said, "Walter Higgins, FBI, coming to my office because a federal magistrate had told him to touch base with me. Higgins was interested in Leon Bascomb, but he said very little about him except that Bascomb was not the name he was born with." He shook his head. "Not much, in fact, as Tony Lopez said later, *muy* damn *poco*. Bascomb was here, a new resident, but so are a bunch of other well-heeled pilgrims. So what, except an FBI man's interest, made him important?"

"Man gave a good party," Ben said. "Good food, good liquor, soft music, pretty girls."

"He was blending in with the community," Johnny said. "Some do; some don't." He shrugged. "But then," he said, and his voice had altered, "Higgins turned up dead on Elk Ridge, apparently dropped from some kind of aircraft. That changed things considerably. Who was Bascomb and why was the FBI interested in him?" He shook his head. "Fact is, the FBI wasn't, only Walter Higgins was. I missed that at first, the possible significance." He paused. "We didn't find out until later that it was a family affair. That explains a lot."

The room was silent.

"But the questions about Bascomb remained," Johnny said. "Who was he? What was he doing here? And why would anybody bother to drop a dead man from an aircraft when the country around here is full of arroyos where the body could have stayed for days, maybe weeks before it was found?"

Ben Hart said, "A weasel in a henhouse. You said that yourself. A killing rage. They happen."

Johnny nodded. "But I didn't follow that up, either, because I couldn't find a connection, any connection. Bascomb was a solid citizen, big house, local investments, well thought of by the right folks. But he drove an armor-plated automobile, Higgins had been killed by an automatic weapon, and Ben saw Bascomb talking to a strange *hombre* out from Miami who, it turned out, thought I'd be better off dead. A lot of things pointed at Bascomb, but we had no proof, none."

Lucille Harrington said, "The numbers on the wristwatch."

"Yes," Johnny said. "Mollie hadn't had them put there, so Higgins must have. And although the numbers looked like a date, it wasn't any date Mollie could account for." He looked at Mollie and the Harringtons. "You three picked that one up and ran with it. I didn't. But the real breakthrough came later when Cassie all of a sudden mentioned Chaco Canyon."

Ben Hart stirred in his chair. "You lost me, boy. Dwell on that."

"It was farfetched," Johnny said, "but finally it had the right feel. A thousand years ago, Chaco Canyon, way out in the middle of nowhere, was a hub, a center."

"And," Cassie said, "we still can't be sure why, but it was."

"So," Johnny said, "what if Santo Cristo, out of the mainstream, was on the way to becoming a kind of center itself? Would that explain why Bascomb was here in the first place? With his obvious connections that could produce a hit man on request, why else would he settle down here in what amounts to a backwater?"

Lucille Harrington said, smiling, "I have said it before. You make intuitive leaps, Johnny."

"Tony Lopez," Cassie said, "claims that he sees visions in smoke." She, too, was smiling. "And I am not sure Tony is entirely wrong."

"Well," Johnny said, "there it was at last, a possibility. The DEA—Drug Enforcement Agency—keeps a close watch on places like Albuquerque, El Paso, Brownsville, Tijuana, obvious places where drugs could, and do, come through. But they mostly ignore us, and why not? It's a 130-mile round trip up and back from I-40, the nearest main east-west route, so why would anyone go that far out of their way to run drugs headed for California? I could only think of a couple of possible answers.

"We don't have real train service, but the Santa Fe station at Lamy is only seventeen miles away. And we do have bus service. And private planes. Were they possibilities? The answer was no. That left only one possibility, and it took me a little time, too much time, to see it." Again he paused.

The room was still.

"Bascomb had investments in the Cadillac dealership," Johnny said. "That's how we learned about the armor plate on his car. And he owned part of a downtown building and was considering investments in other things, too. But he also had a piece of the local moving-van business, and to shorten the story, they had been right on the verge of going broke when Bascomb appeared and bailed them out with a loan. He had moving-van connections in the East, too." He paused for breath.

"We managed," he went on, "to get a look at the van company's computer records showing where all shipments came from and where they were being trans-shipped. Some of the part-loads, too many of them, came from little Gulf Coast towns nobody ever heard of, and were headed for other little towns out on the California desert. From there into L.A. is an easy truck run. Another possibility, no more than that." He shrugged again.

"But this one paid off?" This was Ben Hart.

Johnny nodded. "It did. The DEA head down in Albuquerque called me this morning. Last night they put drug-sniffing dogs on two part-loads out in the California desert. They hit pay dirt with both of them, close to a hundred kilos of cocaine in each load stashed among household goods nobody's ever thought to look hard at before. So they dropped a net over the points of origin on the Gulf Coast and found two stashes, big ones, of drugs that had come ashore by small boats. You'll read about it in the papers or see it on TV tomorrow."

"And that," Lucille Harrington said, "was why Leon Bascomb had come here?" She nodded. "It fits. A quiet place like Santo Cristo, off the beaten path, as you say, with a van and storage company badly needing financial help—" She shook her head. "Ingenious. Mr. Bascomb was the organizer?"

Johnny nodded. "Exactly. But I have a hunch that isn't all. That money in the numbered account tends to argue that Bascomb was skimming funds for himself, in effect working his way out on his own. If that is so, it would also explain the armored car, protection against the Miami mob if they ever found out what he was doing. It would also explain why he came out here himself instead of sending somebody. The DEA thinks drug operations may be moving west, away from Miami, and Bascomb may have been the leading edge." He spread his hands. "There is a lot we will never know. We can only guess."

Ben Hart said, "I can see that because this Higgins dude—excuse me, little lady—got too close, Bascomb killed him. But why the killing rage? Why fly him up to Elk Ridge when he was already dead and drop him from high enough that he'd be all busted up on the talus?"

"Walter," Mollie said, "my husband, was Mr.

Bascomb's brother. The idea that his own brother would try to put him behind bars infuriated him. He as much as said so in my house last night." She paused. Her voice turned apologetic. "He almost seemed insane."

"I think he was, Mollie dear," Lucille said. She made a small, soothing gesture. "I hope you can forget it now, because I have some news for you." She was smiling. "Your security clearance has come through, and you start work Monday, if you are ready, in my section. We will be delighted to have you. I hope you are pleased, too."

"Oh," Mollie said, "I am! Terribly!"

Johnny stifled an incredulous smile. It was, he thought, just another of her bewildering changes of mood.

Mollie's voice turned apologetic again. "It has been a little hard, just waiting, with nothing to do."

"Offhand," Ben Hart said, "I'd say you've been pretty busy, little lady, not really just sitting on your hunkers." He made a gesture of dismissal. "But, then, different folks have different measurements."

Johnny said, "There are still a couple of points." He took his time. "Those numbers you wrote on the paper for Bascomb last night. Were they the real numbers of the bank account?"

"Oh, my, no!" Mollie said. "They were just gibberish. I didn't want the money ever to come into his hands again—if anything had happened." She smiled shyly. "I mean—"

"We know what you mean," Johnny said. "If Ben and I had been a little slow, and he'd gotten away." He nodded. "So now what are you going to do with the bank account?"

"Why," Mollie said, "why, shouldn't the authorities have it? I mean, Mr. Bascomb certainly didn't come by it honestly!"

Johnny nodded again. "Good for you. I talked with Howard, the DEA man, about that this morning, too. They'll be happy to take over the account. No problem, he says. He says something else, too." He was smiling now. "They make a practice of giving rewards. I don't know the percentage, but out of twenty-one million dollars, you are in for a bundle. Congratulations."

"Oh, dear," Mollie said in the shy voice. "I am not sure I could accept that."

"Yes, you will," Lucille Harrington said. "Waldo and I will see that you do. You certainly deserve it."